Heartbreak Trail

BOOKS BY SUSAN MARLOW

Circle C Beginnings
Andi's Pony Trouble
Andi's Indian Summer
Andi's Scary School Days
Andi's Fair Surprise
Andi's Lonely Little Foal
Andi's Circle C Christmas

Circle C Stepping Stones
Andi Saddles Up
Andi Under the Big Top
Andi Lassos Trouble
Andi to the Rescue
Andi Dreams of Gold
Andi Far from Home

Circle C Adventures
Andrea Carter and the Long Ride Home
Andrea Carter and the Dangerous Decision
Andrea Carter and the Family Secret
Andrea Carter and the San Francisco Smugglers
Andrea Carter and the Trouble with Treasure
Andrea Carter and the Price of Truth

Circle C Milestones
Thick as Thieves
Heartbreak Trail
The Last Ride
Courageous Love

Goldtown Beginnings
Jem Strikes Gold
Jem's Frog Fiasco
Jem and the Mystery Thief
Jem Digs Up Trouble
Jem and the Golden Reward
Jem's Wild Winter

Goldtown Adventures
Badge of Honor
Tunnel of Gold
Canyon of Danger
River of Peril

Heartbreak Trail

AN ANDREA CARTER BOOK

Susan K. Marlow

Kregel
Publications

Heartbreak Trail: An Andrea Carter Book
© 2015 by Susan K. Marlow

Published by Kregel Publications, a division of Kregel Inc.,
2450 Oak Industrial Dr. NE, Grand Rapids, MI 49505.

The persons and events portrayed in this work are the creations
of the author, and any resemblance to persons living or dead is
purely coincidental.

Scripture quotations are from the King James Version.

ISBN 978-0-8254-4368-8

Printed in the United States of America
21 22 23 24 25 / 7 6 5 4

Endurance

THE INWARD STRENGTH TO WITHSTAND
HARDSHIP WITHOUT GIVING UP

I can do all things through Christ which strengtheneth me.
Philippians 4:13

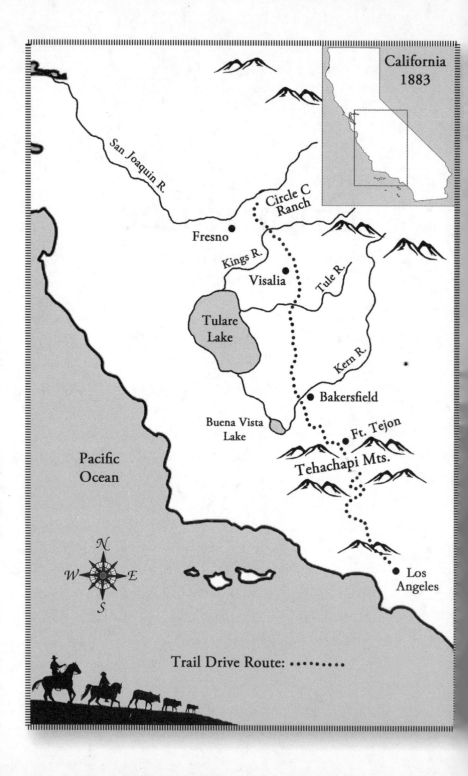

CHAPTER 1

San Joaquin Valley, California, Spring 1883

I thought I was well on my way to outgrowing my penchant for finding trouble. Not so. Ever since Levi showed up at the ranch a month ago, I've discovered that keeping him out of trouble usually backfires and plunges us both smack dab into the middle of a muddle.

Fourteen-year-old Andrea Carter scanned the miles of gullies and scrub-dotted rifts cutting the Sierra foothills and grunted. "Where's that boy got to *now*?" Not for the first time this month, Andi was glad she had older brothers. Younger ones were too much trouble. Levi wasn't her brother, but her sister Kate's son was close enough in age to pester Andi like a little brother might.

Or to get lost?

Her heart skipped at the thought. "Levi!" she hollered for the third time, shading her eyes against the sunshine. "What's taking you so long? Are you lost back there?"

Surely not. The valley was only a mile long and maybe a quarter mile wide, with only one way in or out. Andi sat on Taffy, her palomino mare, near the main trail. The April sun blazed hot and bright, and the brushy thickets lining the creek bottom offered little in the way of shade. The gully did, however, abound with countless hidey-holes for cows and their new calves.

It also held a boy who didn't know as much about being a cowboy as he thought he did.

Anxious to be included in the spring roundup, Andi had offered to help out on Saturdays, promising she'd do anything her brothers asked. Chad had snapped up her offer quicker than a frog after a fly. "Sure, little sister. You and Levi can scout around the draws and root out stragglers. I want to get the last of the calves branded before the drive."

The cattle drive. Andi chewed her lower lip and slumped in the saddle. She had always wanted to go along on a real dust-in-your-face, gone-for-weeks, eat-on-the-trail cattle drive. With at least two thousand cattle. But no matter how often Andi begged, cajoled, and pleaded, the answer was always no.

This year will be different, she vowed. *I'm not a little girl anymore. I don't have to be looked after.* Andi would convince her family she was well able to take care of herself, and also help take care of her family's interests.

She set her jaw in a stubborn line. Mother might as well get used to the fact that Andi was not like her sister Melinda. Ladies' Aid Society meetings and helping out at the orphanage—or finding a beau—were not what Andi wanted to do when she finished school. She wanted to help run the ranch.

Andi shook herself free of her musings. "I better get my head out of the clouds and back to business." She hiked up in her stirrups and hollered, "Levi!"

Levi yahooed his reply from deep inside the canyon, and Andi rolled her eyes. He must have found a cow and her calf. Now, if he would only remember to take it slow and easy, to drive the cow gently and not chase her like he was going after a wild mustang. "Then maybe we can bring them in before sundown," Andi muttered.

She glanced over her shoulder, where a couple dozen shorthorns and their unbranded calves rested in the shade of an oak grove a hundred yards away. They chewed their cuds and swished their tails, while their babies frolicked or napped. Andi had cleared the last of them from their hiding places twenty minutes ago without her horse breaking a sweat. The mamas had plodded ahead of Taffy and settled right down with the rest of Andi's little herd.

Too bad Chad and Mitch can't see me in action. Andi smirked. They'd have to admit she and Taffy were easier on Circle C cattle than some of the rough cowhands. And she always knew where the cows with new calves were hiding.

The thought of her brothers turned Andi's gaze toward the rest of the rounded-up herd. Half a mile away, a wisp of smoke from the branding fire rose into the afternoon sky. Hundreds of cattle milled around in temporary corrals, a dark, lowing smudge against the pale-green foothills.

Andi gritted her teeth. Spring roundup was nearly over, and she'd only helped for three Saturdays. Chad had told her she could brand the calves she brought in today, but now the afternoon was slipping away. She sat astride Taffy waiting for slowpoke Levi, who acted like he didn't know one end of a cow from—

"Levi!" she shouted. "I'm taking my cows to the fire. You can come along when you've a mind to."

Levi didn't answer. He'd either lost his catch and was backtracking up the draw to try again, or he was out of earshot. "It's not like I haven't taught him how to flush strays," she told Taffy. "You'd think he'd—"

A yell loud enough to be heard clear back at the ranch house erupted from the narrow canyon. A large brindle cow burst into view. She splashed across the creek with a days-old calf tight at her flank. Bawling, she threw her head. And no wonder. A rope was looped around one horn.

Levi gripped the other end. "Help!"

Andi jabbed her heels into Taffy's sides and raced toward her nephew. "Let go!" she screamed.

No response. The cow barreled past, dragging Levi along the ground. He was soaking wet, his face set in a look of grim determination mixed with terror. Each time the cow tossed her head, Levi left the ground then landed hard, to be towed farther along.

Horror slammed into Andi, making her gasp. Levi was clutching the rope with both hands, but a good portion of it had somehow entangled itself around one arm. He couldn't free himself, and he dared not loosen his grip. His arm could be torn from its socket.

Just then the spooked cow turned and headed straight for the small herd Andi had spent the last three hours rounding up. They rose and scattered, bellowing their fright. Calves bawled. In no time, most of the cattle had vanished right back into the little canyon. The brindle cow whirled and followed.

Levi shrieked his fear and pain. "Andi! Help!"

In a heartbeat, Andi swiveled her horse and snagged her catch rope. Taffy knew what to do. She edged close to the runaway while Andi circled her lasso. *Please, God*, she prayed as she twirled, *I've got to get her on the first throw. No time for second tries.* If the cow made it back into the draw, Levi might be dragged a full mile through the underbrush and rocky creek bed.

The rope settled neatly over the cow's head, and Andi yanked. The loop tightened. She dallied the rope around the saddle horn, dropped the reins, and clutched the roped horn with both hands.

Taffy stepped back and planted her feet. The catch rope went taut, and mama cow jerked to a bone-jarring stop. Her weight wrenched Andi's rope harder than expected, throwing the mare off balance.

Andi lost her grip on the saddle horn and flipped over Taffy's rump. *Oof!* She landed hard on the ground with the wind knocked out of her. Her heart thudded. She couldn't move. She couldn't breathe.

The world spun. Andi lay still, gasping for breath. Except for the roaring in her ears and the distant mooing of distraught cows scurrying back up the draw, all was still.

Andi lifted her head a minute later when she could finally take a deep breath. Less than twenty feet away, the big brindle cow stood quietly near

Taffy, who kept the catch rope taut and waited for instructions. The calf was nursing.

Mama cow turned her head and looked at Andi as if to say, *Now what?* Levi's rope hung down from one horn and trailed a little way along the ground, ending where a crumpled bulge of brown and blue lay sprawled in the grass.

"Levi!" Andi pushed herself to her hands and knees and crawled over to her nephew. Anger flared. She shook his shoulder. "What were you doing? I've told you a dozen times! You're supposed to find the cows then let Patches take over. *Slow and easy.* Your horse knows what to do." She looked around. "Where is he, anyway?"

Levi sniffled and sat up. The rope, now limp, unwrapped easily from his arm. He tossed it aside, and Andi noticed rope burns on his hands. She winced. They probably burned like fire. Where were his gloves?

"I left Patches in the draw," he confessed. "That dumb ol' cow"—he jerked his chin toward the brindle—"was far back in a thicket. I couldn't get her to budge, no matter what. So I got the rope from Patches and figured I'd—"

"You figured wrong," Andi snapped. She looked around at the empty spot under the oak trees, and her heart sank clear to her dusty boots. "All my hard work today is *gone.*" She whirled, ready to give Levi another piece of her mind. He had it coming.

Levi hung his head. "I'm sorry."

Andi's temper cooled. A few years ago, her unruly nephew would have responded by lighting into her with both fists. He'd clearly grown up some. Right now, he looked beat up. A gash ran across his forehead, dripping blood. His cheeks were grass-stained and crusted with mud. One eye had begun to swell. Andi marveled that he was still in one piece.

"Are you all right?" she asked in a kinder tone. "Anything broken?"

"I don't think so. Just banged up." Levi staggered to his feet with only a little help from Andi. "But I bet I really feel sore tomorrow." He brushed the dirt clods from his britches and looked at her with dark-brown, pleading eyes. "You won't tell Uncle Chad, will you?"

Andi shook her head. "No." She didn't add that Chad would have no trouble figuring it out for himself. It would be mighty hard to cover up this botched job. During each of the past two Saturdays, Andi and Levi had brought in a couple dozen cows and their calves for branding. There was hardly time left in the afternoon to make it up now. Chad probably already wondered where today's quota was.

"Ranch work is harder than I thought," Levi muttered. He kicked at the ground.

"It takes time," Andi reassured him. She didn't have to look down to talk to her nephew. Levi had shot up the past year and matched Andi in height. He probably outweighed her now too. Last month when Kate brought him to the ranch, Levi had been a tall, scraggly-thin scarecrow. A chronic winter cough due to the damp San Francisco air had robbed the twelve-year-old of his energy and appetite.

In no time, the dry, valley climate had cured Levi's cough and restored his health. He followed his uncles everywhere, pestering them to teach him to be a cowhand. Levi worked hard, but apart from the fact he could ride like the wind, most other ranch skills eluded him.

He's a hopeless greenhorn, Andi admitted with a sigh. It was probably the reason Chad saddled her with Levi whenever they weren't in school. "Come on," she said. "We'd best find Patches and round up those . . ." She paused and frowned.

Not far away, a rider on a large, black horse galloped toward them from the direction of the temporary pens and branding fire. Andi shaded her eyes. It wasn't Chad—thank goodness. His horse, Sky, was a showy buckskin.

Andi wasn't ready to face her brother with the news that her little herd had scattered. She'd rather work double time to salvage as many of the cows and calves as she could. They couldn't have strayed far into the canyon. She saw a few drinking at the creek.

The rider drew closer, and Andi groaned. *Uh-oh.*

It was worse than Chad.

CHAPTER 2

Sometimes I think Sid forgets he's our foreman and not our father. We all love him dearly, but I get mighty tired of listening to his advice, even when he's right.

In less than a minute, the rider caught up. He reined his black gelding up so short it almost sat down. Then he glanced around and quickly assessed the situation.

"What in tarnation's goin' on here?" he demanded, narrowing his eyes at Levi's rumpled appearance.

Andi felt heat creep into her cheeks. Of all the cowhands Chad could send, why did he choose Sid McCoy to check up on her? Old and grizzled but still spry as a colt, Sid had helped Chad run the ranch ever since Father passed away nine years ago. His advice and experience were invaluable, but Sid didn't agree with Chad's decision to let Andi help out, and he didn't care who knew it. Lately, his disapproval had become even more vocal.

Today's bungling would give Sid plenty of ammunition the next time he complained to Chad.

When Andi didn't answer, the ranch foreman shoved his hat back off his forehead and nodded toward the area under the oak trees. "I recollect seeing cattle in that spot not more'n twenty minutes ago," he growled. "Chad's waitin' on the stock you and the boy was s'posed to be fetchin'."

I reckon he'll just have to wait a little longer, Andi thought, but she held her tongue.

Sid swung out of his saddle, walked over to the brindle cow, and loosened the ropes from around her neck and one horn. Taffy shook her mane and started grazing.

"It don't take much figurin' to guess what happened." Sid's gray eyes flashed. "You got no business bangin' up your horse's knees like that. She ain't no cow pony to go up against a full-growed cow. You're s'posed to be *drivin'* cows, not ropin' 'em."

"Taffy's fine." Andi squirmed under the barb. "She dug in with her back legs, just like Chad and I taught her." Did Sid think she couldn't manage her own horse? "Besides, what choice did I have? I couldn't let the cow drag Levi clear across the range." She brightened. "I caught her on my first throw."

Sid snorted his disbelief. "I told your brother it wasn't a good idea to let a gal handle—"

"I'll go after the cows," Andi cut in, peeved. She wished Sid would mind his own business.

"No need. I got it covered." Sid gave a sharp whistle then raised his hat and circled it above his head. Two small shapes broke off from the main crew and headed their way. When the cowhands drew near, Sid gestured toward the ravine. The men pivoted and took off.

Andi slumped. No calf branding for her today.

"It's not Andi's fault." Levi eyed the foreman with distrust. "I bungled things and scattered the herd. Andi only tried to—"

"I don't doubt it." Sid chuckled. He looked Levi up and down then clapped him on the shoulder. "Sometimes it takes a tumble or two to learn your business. If you ain't too beat up you can go along with Diego and Flint and help find the cows that got away."

"I'm not too beat up, but Uncle Chad made Andi my boss today." Levi glared at the foreman out of his good eye. "*She* tells me what to do."

Andi wanted to hug her nephew for his support. It took pluck to stand up to Sid these days. The usually jovial foreman had turned prickly and short-tempered the past year. Maybe his age was catching up with him.

Sid brushed off Levi's backtalk with a grin. "Suit yourself, boy." He tousled Levi's hair and thumbed toward the old cow now grazing quietly next to Taffy. "That's a lot o' cow to rope."

"Yes, sir," Levi mumbled.

Sid turned to Andi and crossed his arms. His smile vanished. "As for *you*, missy. You're gettin' too old to be playin' at cowboy. It mighta been all right when you was a little gal, but it ain't fittin'—"

"I'm *not* playing," Andi said between clenched teeth. "I'm working." Sid laughed off Levi's botched job but dressed her down for saving her nephew's life? *No fair!* "Besides, Chad's the boss." This last came out as a whisper. Talking back to Sid made her stomach turn over. It felt a little like talking back to Father if he were alive.

Happily for Andi, Sid's hearing wasn't what it used to be. "What's that?"

Andi shrugged. "Nothing."

Sid took Andi by the shoulders and forced her to look at him. His wrinkled, weather-beaten expression softened. "I ain't riled at you, Miss Andi," he said. "It ain't your fault your ma don't stick to her guns. I expect you just plumb wore her down with wantin' to ride and rope and brand critters all the time."

Andi raised her eyebrows. Is *that* what he thought? If so, Sid McCoy did not know Elizabeth Carter very well. Andi hadn't yet been able to talk her way around Mother once she made up her mind. If she hadn't given her say-so, Andi would not be out on roundup with Levi today, or any day.

Andi forced her attention back to Sid's gravelly voice. He'd loosened his grip on her shoulders and was now embroiled in the past. "Your family's been good to me, Miss Andi. Your pa hired me long before you was born. Me, a widower with a little, three-year-old girl to raise."

Andi listened with one ear. She'd heard this story too many times. Beside her, Levi heaved a sigh. *Bet he's wishing he'd gone after the cows.*

"I've worked for your family nigh onto twenty years. I mourned when your pa lost his life in that terrible accident. I've watched your brothers grow up into fine young men. Justin's a first-rate lawyer, and Chad and Mitch have turned this ranch into one of the finest spreads in California. Your ma's the most respected woman around these parts . . ."

. . . And Melinda's the sweetest young lady in the valley, Andi added silently. She swallowed her laughter when Sid said those very words, but a giggle sneaked out.

Sid waggled his finger in Andi's face. "Don't you go laughing at me, Miss Andi. I'm downright serious. Been meanin' to pull you aside lately and have a word with you, now that Justin's married and not around to advise you as much as he used to." He paused. "I hear tell your family's throwin' you a fancy *quinceañera* when you turn fifteen next month. Ain't that some sorta milestone 'tween childhood and becoming a growed-up woman?"

Andi nodded. Sid's words rang true, at least for the Mexicans and the Spanish *Californios.* It made Andi's head spin to think how fast Rosa had grown up over the past several months. Her best friend had no sooner celebrated her *quinceañera* when Hector from the neighboring Bent Pine ranch came calling. Now, a year later, Rosa was promised in marriage. She'd leave the Circle C for good in the fall.

Rosa's loco. She's only sixteen.

Andi roused herself. *Quinceañera*s and birthdays aside, it was not Sid's duty to point any of this out to her. He wasn't Father. Or Justin. She shifted impatiently from one foot to the other and glanced toward the canyon. Diego emerged with a cow and calf. Flint followed right behind with another pair.

"I could've rounded up half those cows by now," she said. "Instead, you're filling my ears with all kinds of nonsense about—"

"You gotta get this silly notion 'bout ranchin' outta your head," Sid interrupted. "Your family's got a reputation to uphold. Carter young ladies don't flush strays or challenge the cowhands to lassoing contests."

Andi scowled. "Why not?" Just last week she'd beat Flint in one such contest. He'd been a good sport about it, so what was the harm? "Chad says I can ride and rope just as well as—"

"I respect your brother like I respected your pa," Sid broke in again. "Chad's a good rancher—one of the best around—but he gives in too easy when it comes to *you*, Miss Andi."

Andi laughed out loud. Was Sid joking? Chad, give in to *her*? No, Chad never played favorites when it came to running the ranch. She'd earned her right to help out fair and square. "If I couldn't do the job, Chad would make sure I didn't get the chance."

Sid didn't look convinced. "I've told Chad over an' over, but he don't listen to me. If the hands treat you like one of their own, you'll eventually get hurt. And if they remember you're not only a girl but one of the family, they'll get hurt trying to keep you out of danger."

Andi looked around. She and Levi worked alone. Chad never let her work with the rest of the outfit unless he or Mitch was right there. She started to say as much, but Sid drew his bushy, gray eyebrows together in warning. Andi clamped her mouth shut and silently stewed.

"Another thing." Sid waved his hand at her attire. "You're too pretty to go around lookin' like a poor no-account. Look at you. Sloppy braids, a raggedy shirt, and those dusty, unnatural britches."

"They're not britches. It's a split skirt and perfectly acceptable."

Sid grunted. "It ain't fittin'."

So you say. Andi pressed her lips together.

The foreman took a deep breath. "You're like my own daughter, Miss Andi, and I'm tellin' you: Girls goin' on fifteen gotta start lookin' and behavin' like young ladies. They need to brush and comb their hair all purty to catch a beau—"

"I'm not interested in catching a beau," Andi blurted, face burning. Up till now, Sid had been rambling. Now he was meddling. Two more cows and calves plodded past.

Levi tittered. Andi elbowed him into silence. He grunted and rubbed his side.

"Maybe you ain't interested right now," Sid went on. "But it don't hurt none to practice now and then. You could take a lesson from Miss Melinda—"

"You talk worse than Aunt Rebecca." Andi'd had it up to her eyebrows. "Did she put you up to this? Did she pay you to badger me?"

Levi burst out laughing. Their Aunt Rebecca's reputation for propriety was well known in both her San Francisco mansion and on the Circle C. "He does sound like Auntie, doesn't he?" Levi doubled over in mirth then groaned. "It hurts too much to laugh."

Sid did not laugh. He whipped off his hat and slapped it against his leg. Dust flew everywhere. "Doggone it, you two. That does it! Don't you insult me by comparing me to that ol' peahen—"

Levi gasped.

In a heartbeat, the old foreman's demeanor changed. He stood stock-still. Slowly, he replaced his hat, took out his bandana, and wiped his red, sweaty face. Then he cleared his throat. "You gone and done it now. You riled me up so much I forgot myself and spoke my mind without thinkin'."

Andi knew Sid meant well. But honestly! "I only wanted to—"

"I apologize, Miss Andi." Sid backed up stiffly. "I was outta line. I reckon it ain't my place to tell you these things. That's your ma's job, or maybe Justin's the next time he comes around." Without another word, he stalked to his horse and climbed into the saddle.

Andi watched him. All anger at Sid's attempt to send her home for a pretty frock dissolved when she saw how worn out he looked. The foreman might mount as fast as any youngster, but the long workdays of this year's roundup were clearly taking their toll. He pulled his horse around and shouted at Diego and Flint.

Andi followed his hollering and cringed. No wonder Sid was yelling. Flint couldn't seem to handle cattle any better than Levi. She shook her head. "C'mon, Levi. Let's find Patches and the last of the cows. I bet I know right where they're hiding."

Sid whirled and flung one last remark at Andi about keeping out of his way. Then he slammed his heels into his mount and galloped back toward the branding fire and the rest of the herd.

Levi found his hat, scooped up the loose rope, and followed Andi to Taffy. When he'd mounted up behind her he gave a loud sigh. "I guess this wouldn't be a very good time to ask if you can go on the cattle drive."

Andi swallowed the boulder-sized lump that had settled in her throat. "You're right, Levi," she said. "Not a good time at *all*."

CHAPTER 3

*It took some doing, but I have scoured
newspapers from San Francisco to Kansas City
(and every city in between) to find clippings about
spirited women who balked at society's expectations
and mounted their horses to follow their own
dreams. Levi says it's like looking for a needle in
our hayloft. He's right.*

Andi closed her journal and leaned back against the wall in Taffy's stall. Instead of stuffing the book behind the feedbox, she held it against her chest and sent up a heartfelt prayer. "Please convince Mother to at least *listen* to my idea tonight." She'd filled three pages with fine script, copying important facts from old newspapers the townsfolk had given her. She'd also cut out articles and slipped them between her journal pages for safekeeping.

"It's a cockeyed, hopeless plan," Levi had muttered the day before, when a two-foot stack of newspapers yielded only four worthwhile clippings. "My eyes are crossing."

After a week of searching pages and pages of tiny print, Andi's eyes felt gritty and sore too, but she couldn't give up. Not when her brothers would soon be heading out on the cattle drive.

"It's my one chance to go along," Andi now told her mare. Although she adored Taffy's yearling colt, Shasta, it was Taffy in whom she always confided. "The drive will last less than three weeks—just a short hop to Los Angeles. There's no reason I shouldn't go along." She pulled herself to her feet and slapped Taffy on the rump. "I reckon it's now or never, girl. I'm going to ask tonight."

Taffy turned her golden head toward Andi and nickered. She looked eager to go along with whatever her mistress had in mind.

"I'll let you know how it turns out," Andi promised.

She left the barn just as the supper bell rang for the cowhands. Whooping and laughing, three men barely missed colliding with Andi as they sprinted past. They waved their apologies and slammed through the cookhouse door.

Andi hurried up the back porch steps and through the kitchen entrance of the Circle C's two-story, hacienda-styled ranch house. She didn't want to be late for supper tonight. No sirree! She'd planned everything down to the tiniest detail, hoping to convince her mother to let her go along on the drive. Showing up late at the table was not part of the plan, nor was appearing in a tattered state and smelling like a horse.

The good news was that Justin and his young wife, Lucy, had joined the family for dinner after church, like they often did, and weren't returning to town until after supper.

"Having Justin around the table is always a plus," Andi told herself as she scrubbed her hands at the kitchen pump. Then she scurried upstairs to change clothes and brush her hair.

Supper progressed just as Andi hoped it would. Lucy and Melinda chatted about fashions and box socials, while Chad and Mitch argued over the details of the upcoming cattle drive. *Perfect timing.* A few minutes more and—

"It's a little over a month away, Andrea, and you haven't yet told us what you'd like to do for your *quinceañera*."

The unexpected question halfway through supper jerked Andi from her careful planning. She scrambled to focus her attention on her mother's words. "What?"

Elizabeth Carter smiled. "Luisa and Nila are fussing. They can't wait to begin preparations for the *fiesta*."

The little-girl-to-grown-up-woman milestone, Andi thought in dismay. Why did Mother have to bring that up *now*? Andi didn't want to talk about her birthday celebration this evening, no matter how important it might be to the hired help. They were always eager for a party. One of the family turning fifteen was sure to involve *una gran fiesta*—an affair even grander and longer-lasting than Rosa's *quinceañera* last year.

Andi felt for the journal lying under the napkin in her lap and squeezed it. Mother's question had piqued the whole family's interest. Lucy and Melinda glanced up, faces bright with curiosity. The boys dropped their cattle-drive discussion and listened. Levi stopped chewing. Everybody looked at Andi.

I don't want to think about my birthday right now. I want to . . .

A sudden, splendid idea bubbled up, making Andi catch her breath. The words burst from her mouth before she could snatch them back. "I want to go along on the cattle drive next week."

Stunned silence greeted her announcement. Levi choked on a mouthful of dumplings and reached for his milk. Over the rim of the glass, his eyes glittered their surprise at Andi's boldness.

Tingles raced up and down Andi's spine. This was not the way she'd planned to bring up the subject, but Mother's question seemed like a heaven-sent opportunity. *After all, she asked me what I wanted to do.*

Before Elizabeth could express her surprise, Andi blurted, "Why can't I drive cattle just once? *You* brought the herd down from the high country, remember?"

"She's got you there, Grandmother," Levi piped up, setting his milk aside. A white mustache covered his upper lip.

Elizabeth frowned at her grandson. "Use your napkin." Then she turned to Andi. "That was thirty-five years ago and a terrible experience. Your father and I waited too late in the fall to go after the cattle. We were young and unfamiliar with the fickleness of the Sierras. We didn't count on an early blizzard. If it hadn't been for that old prospector's cabin—"

"—that you two stumbled across in the nick of time," Chad cut in, "none of us would be here."

Andi snickered. Mother loved to tell stories of the "olden days," when she and Father worked hard together to make something grand out of their new spread. Good fortune in the gold fields had given Father the means to buy the Circle C, but they couldn't afford to lose any cattle. They risked their lives more than once bringing the tiny herd down from the high country to winter in the valley.

By the time Elizabeth finished her tale, everyone was chuckling.

Andi plunged on. "This trail drive won't be going anywhere *near* a snowflake, Mother. Besides, it's—"

"Snow is not my concern," Elizabeth interrupted. "I'm retelling that well-worn blizzard story to remind you that there is always the unexpected to contend with. Driving cattle is hard work, as I well know."

"Not to mention how unseemly it would be," Melinda put in. "A young lady on a cattle drive? The very idea!"

Leave it to Melinda to bring that up. Andi held her tongue with difficulty. She wanted to lash out at her sister, but losing her temper would set Mother on edge. Andi wanted to keep her place at the table tonight, so she swallowed her *keep out of this!* and silently counted to twenty in Spanish.

When her temper still hadn't cooled, she counted backward in French. *If only Peter Wilson would hurry up and ask for Melinda's hand in marriage.* Then Melinda would be too busy planning a wedding to nag Andi about what a young lady should or shouldn't be doing.

She let out a disheartened sigh. "You asked me what I wanted to do for my *quinceañera*, so I told you."

"I think Mother expected a different answer," Melinda said brightly. "Like a leisurely trip by rail to the city, not a plodding trek south in the company of a thousand balky steers." She made a face.

"I've been to the city," Andi said abruptly. "I never want to see it again."

Silence fell. The family needed no reminder of Andi's regrettable stay in San Francisco two years ago. Melinda shrugged and went back to her discussion with Lucy. Supper conversation resumed.

Andi slumped. Her birthday wish was out in the open now. At least Mother hadn't said no right off. There was still hope. She let the table talk swirl around her and listened with only half an ear.

It was the same old thing. Chad and Mitch were arguing over who would be trail boss and who would ramrod the outfit. The trail boss took charge of everything: the cowboys, the cattle herd, the chuck wagon, and keeping the records. The ramrod was second in command. He made sure the trail boss's orders were followed, and that the whole drive went smoothly.

It was no trick for Andi to figure out who would land the trail-boss position: Chad Carter, the big boss of anybody he could find.

Clink!

Andi started and glanced up from her supper. A silver dollar had hit her knife and now lay next to her plate. Before anyone could blink, she slapped her hand over it.

"What is it?" Chad demanded from across the table. "Heads or tails?"

"Wouldn't *you* like to know," Andi replied with a saucy grin. She lifted her palm slightly and peeked at the coin. Heads. *I wonder if Chad and Mitch decided to flip for trail boss.* It would be a first.

Andi's heart leaped at the thought. Had Chad softened enough to let Mitch boss the outfit if he won the toss? If so, would he be willing to consider including his youngest sister on the drive . . . just this once?

"Cut it out, Andi," Mitch said from where he sat next to Chad. He held out his palm. "Hand it over. We'll toss it again."

Andi shook her head.

Chad lunged across the table for the coin. Laughing, Andi held it out of his reach. Melinda giggled.

Even Mother was smiling. "I think we need an attorney to mediate this dispute," she suggested.

Justin laughed. "Not *this* lawyer." He winked at Andi. It was his good-for-you look, which meant that for once Andi might end up having the last word.

Andi held the coin hostage for another few moments before giving in. Deep down, she knew the coin toss was probably just a polite gesture on Chad's part. He and Mitch would run things together no matter who won. Flipping a coin most likely decided who would be blamed—and ribbed—if and when things went wrong.

"I'll tell you how it landed if you let me keep the dollar," Andi said.

"You can keep it," Mitch said.

Chad punched his arm. "Hey, it's *my* dollar." Then he relented. "Sure, sis, you can keep it."

Andi grinned. "All right then. It was heads."

Mitch let out a loud, "Yee-*haw!*"

I'd grin and holler too, if I were Mitch, Andi thought sourly. She wished earning a place on the drive was as simple as flipping a coin. *Heads I go; tails I stay home.*

Andi shuddered. *No, too chancy.*

She needed a surefire way of securing herself a spot on the short jaunt to southern California. Perhaps what she'd discovered in the newspaper clippings would be the key that unlocked Mother's resistance and opened the door to this new adventure.

CHAPTER 4

Everybody should have a big brother like Justin. I honestly don't know what I would do without him. I feared that once he married, he'd vanish from my life. But no! He still takes time to help me out, just like Father would do if he were alive.

With the coin toss decided, Mitch and Chad shook hands. "All right, little brother," Chad gave in gracefully. "You can boss the outfit this time. I'll be your humble ramrod and boss everybody else. I hate keeping the herd records anyway."

"That's certainly true," Justin quipped, which brought a round of chuckles.

Through the years, Andi had enjoyed numerous tales at her brother's expense about his poor school record. It had taken a lot of arguments and their father's firm hand to keep hard-headed Chad Carter in school until age sixteen.

But nobody knew practical ranching better. Andi was confident Chad could even bring Circle C cattle safely through an anthrax epidemic if need be, with or without Dr. Pasteur's fancy new medicine called a "vaccine."

Chad and Mitch bantered back and forth while Andi scooped a huge helping of dried-peach cobbler Luisa had set on the table right next to her. Between mouthfuls of hot, sweet peaches and crusty cobbler, Andi listened to the trail boss ask his new ramrod a few questions about the dozen or so hands they'd be bringing along.

"I hired half a dozen drovers in town yesterday," Mitch said. "That way most of our own hands can stay home." He chuckled. "You know how cranky Sid gets when he's shorthanded."

Sid's cranky about everything these days, Andi put in silently.

Chad nodded his approval. "What about the wrangler?"

Andi looked up with interest. A cattle drive needed someone to care for the *remuda*—the forty or fifty extra horses they'd bring along. A cowboy would ride four or five mounts during his long, dusty shift. *I could wrangle the horses*, Andi mused, blowing on her forkful of cobbler.

"I snagged young Flint," Mitch said.

Andi's fork stopped halfway to her mouth. "Flint? Flint *Hadley*, the new hand? Why, he's greener than . . . than Levi." She flicked her nephew an apologetic look. He shrugged as if this was no news to him.

"Andrea," Mother warned. *Stay out of this* flashed from her eyes.

Andi couldn't stay out of it. "I can handle horses better than Flint. I watched him pick his string last month. It took him three tries to get a rope around his mount. By then, the whole *remuda* was spooked and running around the corral like a carousel. He didn't do any better last Saturday going after those cows Levi scattered."

She popped the cobbler in her mouth and swallowed. "Why don't you hire *me* on as wrangler? You wouldn't even have to pay me. Think how much money you'd save."

Chad rolled his eyes at Andi's suggestion. "I know Flint's a little green," he told Mitch. "But this would be a good first run for him."

Mitch nodded. "What about Cook?" He looked like he was crossing off names on a mental checklist. "I think he should stay home. He's got that bum knee and is getting on in years. Marty could go instead."

Chad chuckled. "You do that, and Cook will walk off this ranch. You know he's the most experienced *hombre* of the entire crew. He's cooked for this spread since you and I were knee-high to bumblebees, and he's never missed a drive." He shook his head and dug into his cobbler. "I'm not fool enough to insult Cook like that. But hey, boss, you go right ahead and do what you think best."

Mitch elbowed Chad and grudgingly agreed. "All right, but we should find a boy to fetch and carry for him." He furrowed his brow. "Joselito used to do that, but he's working cattle now."

Andi felt her impatience rise. All this talk about hiring a boy when—

Wait a minute! Cook's helper didn't sound like much fun, and she'd rather be a cowhand or a wrangler, but if a little boy could help Cook, then it must be pretty safe. "Say, Mitch," Andi said. "What if—"

"Why don't you take Levi along as Cook's helper?" Justin's words fell like a cannon shot.

Levi? Andi gaped at Justin as if he'd lost his mind.

Levi gasped and dropped his fork. It clattered to his plate. Bits of peach splattered onto the tablecloth. *"Me?"* His eyes sparkled with eagerness. "I'm not much use with cattle, but I know how to tote firewood and water." He gave his grandmother a pleading look. "Can I? I'm sure Mama would say it's fine."

Like Andi, Levi knew who had the final say in any cattle-drive plans.

"I agree," Elizabeth said after a long minute. "I think it would be a good experience, especially since your health has been restored this past month. I'll write Katherine and let her know." She smiled at Levi.

"Sounds good to me," Mitch agreed.

"Yippee!" Levi whooped. "You won't be sorry, Uncle Mitch. I'll do my best for you and Cook."

Mitch winked. "I know you will, partner."

A sick knot formed in Andi's stomach. Levi had been *her* faithful partner all month, helping her plan how she'd wrangle her way onto the cattle drive. Now, with one offhand suggestion from Justin, Levi was going instead. *And I'm no closer to going than I was a month ago.*

Andi drew her journal out from under the table. Desperation made her speak up quickly, before Mitch and Chad decided anything more. She couldn't be left behind! "Mother," she said, "I'm serious about going along on this cattle drive. Will you and the boys please hear me out?"

Silence settled over the table.

"Andi's done a jim-dandy job finding all kinds of stories—" Levi began.

"I've learned about many young women in the West who are just as successful as the men," Andi said, giving Levi a frown. She brought out the clippings and a fuzzy newspaper photograph. "This is Kitty Wilkins. She and her brothers run a ranch up in Idaho Territory. She rounds up wild horses right alongside the ranch hands and sells them. She goes to the stockyards and does the trading herself, and she isn't even married."

Melinda and Lucy gasped.

Andi grinned. She had everybody's attention now. "When she's done selling the mustangs, Kitty dresses up and goes to fancy restaurants and to the theater. Nobody guesses she was out on the range only weeks before." She flipped through the clippings. "The *San Francisco Examiner* calls her the 'Horse Queen of Idaho.'"

"I've heard of Miss Wilkins," Mother said. She glanced at the picture of the beautiful lady riding sidesaddle on her horse. "She's vastly ahead of her time. She retains her femininity and is a lady through and through, despite her unusual occupation."

Andi thrust another clipping toward her mother. "Here's another lady who helps run her ranch and even registered her own brand. Lizzie Williams and her husband drive their herds together along the Chisholm Trail."

Melinda's eyebrows arched. "Seriously? This Lizzie woman participates in a *cattle drive*?"

"She sure does." Andi turned the pages of her journal. "I have other examples too. I took three pages of notes." She closed the journal and held it out. "Please read it, Mother."

Elizabeth took Andi's journal with a smile. "I will," she promised.

Andi's heart fluttered. For an instant, she saw a faraway look in her mother's eyes, as if she was remembering that a certain Elizabeth Carter was once a young woman helping her husband start up their ranch.

"Your point?" Chad broke in with a grin. By the look on his face, he already knew Andi's point and was ready to agree with her.

"We're not living in the old days any longer—or back East either," Andi said. "It's 1883 and almost a new century." She nodded at the journal in her mother's hand. "I wanted to show you that there are many courageous women who don't go along with what society expects of them. Instead, they do what they love and still remain ladies."

Andi's throat tightened. *I will not cry.* "I can be like Kitty Wilkins, Mother. I can still be a lady and do what I think God put inside me to do, what I love to do. I'm good at it too." She turned to Chad. "Aren't I?"

"That you are," Chad admitted.

For a full minute nobody said a word. Melinda's blue eyes were round with surprise, but Lucy was smiling. When she caught Andi's worried glance, she winked—just like Justin always did. Mother glanced through the clippings and photographs.

Andi held her breath and waited. Saying anything more at this point might tip her words into begging, and that could easily backfire.

Justin cleared his throat, and his words sent Andi's spirit leaping for joy. "You ought to let her go, Mother. Andi's presented an exceptional case, and I think you know it. I remember as little boys Chad and I rode with you and Father to round up cattle in the spring and fall. You could handle the herd with the best of them."

"That's true," Elizabeth agreed with a reluctant sigh. But her eyes betrayed her thoughts: How could she keep her daughter from doing what she herself had done years ago?

"If nothing else," Justin added, chuckling, "she'll get this cattle-drive notion out of her head once and for all."

Andi bit down hard on her lip to keep from shouting a hearty *yahoo!*

"Cook will keep an eye on Andi and Levi better than Chad and Mitch combined," Justin continued. "She's safe enough with the chuck wagon." He turned to Andi. "You'll learn firsthand, young lady, that a cattle drive is not a holiday. It's a lot of hot, dirty, long—not to mention monotonous—days, and even longer nights. When you come back, I expect you'll never ask to participate in a trail drive again."

"I expect she'll wish she'd chosen something different for her *quinceañera*," Melinda remarked.

Andi gave her sister a dirty look. *We'll see about that.*

Justin's sensible words persuaded their mother. "I am not excited about the idea, Andrea," she said. "But if Mitch and Chad are willing to take you along, and *if* you stay with the chuck wagon, then I have no objections." She paused. "This once."

"Don't worry, Mother," Chad said. "If Andi wearies of the hard work and dust after a week, Mitch and I will put her on the train at Bakersfield and send her home."

"I have no plans to wear myself out," Andi retorted. "In fact . . ." Her words trailed away at the look on her mother's face. She gulped. "I mean, sure, Chad. That sounds like a good idea, just in case." She pasted a smile on her face, but her eyes shot daggers at her brother.

Chad chuckled, clearly happy to have baited her into reacting.

Andi pushed Chad's teasing from her mind and leaped from her seat. She threw her arms around her mother's neck. "Thank you!" She kissed her cheek then rushed over to Justin, who had risen from the table with Lucy to take their leave. "Thank *you*, Justin!" Andi squeezed him hard.

Justin hugged her back. "I doubt you'll be thanking me a week from now."

Andi was too excited to worry about a week from now. She pinched herself to make sure she wasn't dreaming.

I'm really and truly going on a cattle drive!

*Getting ready for a cattle drive is a lot of work—
more than I expected. Worse, there's no pleasing
Cook. He acts like he wishes I wasn't going
along. That hurts, but I won't be talked out of
this trip, not by Cook or by anybody else.*

The thousand cattle headed for market in Los Angeles were cut out of the
herd and rounded up in a quivering mass of bawling, unhappy steers two
miles from the ranch house. Andi had nothing to do with them. Neither
did Levi. They had their own work to finish, and it could only be accom-
plished after school or during the weekend before the drive started.

On the Saturday before they headed out, Cook kept Andi and Levi
hopping from dawn till dusk.

Levi was in the middle of scrubbing the last of a dozen pots and pans
Cook insisted must shine like silver dollars. "The fire'll blacken them all
over again the first time he uses them. Why's he suddenly so particular
about these ol' pots?" Levi peered into a large Dutch oven and shook his
head. "This one can't be polished. It's cast iron." He set it aside and picked
up a heavy frying pan. "So's this skillet. What's Cook thinking?"

Andi pulled Levi aside and hushed him. "Cook's thinking if he works
us hard enough he might change our minds about going. I heard him tell
Mitch he doesn't want to be saddled with us—or with any so-called 'help.'
Says he doesn't need it."

She eyed the old Mexican hobbling toward them. A length of stripped deadwood under one arm served as a makeshift crutch. His other arm encircled a toolbox of blacksmithing tools for horseshoeing and horse tack repair. He heaved it onto the chuck wagon and grimaced.

"Looks to me like he needs plenty of help." Levi kept his voice low, but Cook had exceptional hearing.

He whirled on Levi. *"No, chico. No necesito ayuda,"* he growled. He shoved the toolbox into its rightful place on the compact wagon.

In addition to repair equipment, cooking gear, and foodstuffs, the chuck wagon was packed tightly with every imaginable item the cowhands might need on the trail. Cook picked up a rolled-up cloth that held sewing needles and thread for mending torn clothing. He stashed it in a cubbyhole next to his box of medicines and home remedies.

Scowling, he thumbed toward the far side of the wagon. *"Hay agua?"*

Andi nodded. There was plenty of water. The other side of the chuck wagon held a large wooden barrel, which Levi had filled with a two-day supply for cooking and drinking. Underneath the wagon, a hammock-like piece of canvas called the "possum belly" carried the first day's supply of firewood.

Cook grunted and sent a stream of impatient Spanish in Levi's direction. Since Levi didn't speak the language, he ignored Cook. For the first time in her life, Andi wished *she* didn't speak it either. Cook's complaints were beginning to wear on her nerves.

An hour later, Cook's left leg collapsed under a fifty-pound sack of flour he was lugging. Andi and Levi were rewarded for helping him with a gruff *"¡Vayanse!"*

Andi was only too happy to go away.

Mitch motioned to her from across the yard. "Don't pay Cook's grumbling any mind," he advised when she joined him. "Respect him and help him as much as you can, but try not to make it look like you're helping too much."

"But *you* hired Levi and me," Andi protested. "He might as well accept it."

"He's old and he's proud," Mitch said. "It's not easy for him to admit he needs help, especially from a gi—" Mitch cleared his throat. "Never mind. I have it on the best authority that Cook likes you. He and Sid are just a couple of old-timers. They can't understand why we're allowing you to dabble in ranch activities." He laughed.

Andi didn't think it was funny.

"Don't take it to heart, sis. Give Cook a few days on the trail and he'll get over it." Mitch tugged affectionately at her braid. "I don't think he and Sid like the idea of a youngster like me being trail boss either, but they can gripe all they like. They'll eventually come around and accept the way things are. I promise."

Mitch's words smoothed Andi's ruffled feathers. She grinned at the thought of Cook calling Mitch a youngster. He was twenty-four years old and had been running the ranch for nearly as long as Chad had.

The sound of pounding hooves brought them both around. Mitch shaded his eyes. "I gotta go and welcome the new hands. We'll rest tomorrow and head out bright and early Monday." He crossed the yard to meet a half dozen riders reining in their mounts. "You can turn your horses into the large corral," he hollered.

Andi ambled across the yard after him.

The new hands were young. Only one or two looked over the age of eighteen. They greeted their boss with boisterous howdies, clearly eager to have this trail job, even if it only lasted a couple of weeks. "We hear the Circle C serves up the best chuck this side o' the Sierras," one scruffy, freckle-faced boy said.

"Very true, Bryce. So long as you stay on Cook's good side," Mitch bantered back.

They laughed.

Off to one side of the group, a tall, good-looking cowboy sat his horse as if he were leading a rodeo procession. Andi caught her breath. The horse was at least sixteen hands tall and held his head high. His black mane and tail stood out against his glistening white body.

He's gorgeous! Andi thought. *Not your ordinary cow pony.* She couldn't help wondering if the horse was any good at rounding up maverick steers. He seemed more suited for a parade than for a cattle drive.

The cowboy also held his head high. He acted more serious than the other drovers, though he was not much older. His clothes were clean and pressed instead of trail-worn. He caught Andi gaping at him and swept off his hat.

"Howdy-do, miss," he called to her in a pleasant voice, nodding politely. A wide smile showed even, white teeth.

Andi blushed. *Not just any cowboy, either.* She returned his nod.

When the new drovers dismounted and shook hands with Mitch, the tall cowboy stayed in his saddle. He surveyed the ranch with sparkling, black eyes. "I want to get settled straightaway," he told Mitch. "Where's the bunkhouse?"

Mitch waved at Levi, who had come up beside Andi to watch. "Levi, show Toledo where he can stow his gear, will you?"

"Sure thing," Levi said, goggling at the circus spectacle. "This way, mister." He led the way past the round pen and behind the blacksmith shed.

Andi flicked a hurried glance at the other five cowhands, who were chattering and yanking their saddles from their dusty mounts. Then she took off after Levi to get a closer look at the white stallion. *Maybe this Toledo fellow will let me ride his horse if I ask nicely,* she thought.

Andi caught up to Levi and Toledo as they rounded the blacksmith shop. "That pretty little filly your sister?" she heard Toledo ask. She stopped in mid-step and hung back to keep out of sight. A tingle crept along her spine at the cowboy's bold words.

Levi looked up at the rider towering over him. "No, she's my—"

"Is the boss your pa?"

"Who, Mitch?" Levi laughed. "Somethin' wrong with your eyes, mister? He's not old enough to be my pa. He's—"

"Where's the bunkhouse?" Toledo cut in, ignoring Levi's jab.

"Over there." Levi pointed to the blue-gray building just beyond the blacksmith shed. "Likely there's a good bunk or two left." He turned on his heel to go.

"Hey, whoa, boy," Toledo ordered.

Levi stiffened and slowly turned to face Toledo.

The new cowhand smiled pleasantly. "How 'bout lugging my stuff inside?"

Andi held her breath. It was worded nicely, but if Levi let Toledo boss him once, he'd keep doing it. *Should I warn him?* No, Levi had to stand up for himself. And he wouldn't like it if she interfered.

Levi had no trouble speaking his mind. "Do it yourself." His clenched fists told Andi that although her nephew had matured considerably the last couple of years, his rough edges still lingered near the surface. "My uncles give the orders around here."

"That so?" Toledo answered, not missing a beat. "Well, when they're not around, I'll see to it." With that, he popped Levi with the knotted end of a rope he was carrying. "See?" The *crack* caught Levi across the shoulders. He yelped and ducked, just missing the next snap.

Andi gasped at Toledo's rattlesnake-quick reaction. Levi may have deserved a cuff for his sass, but not that way, and certainly not from a hired hand. She took a step forward.

Sid appeared in the bunkhouse doorway. "What's the ruckus?" he demanded, stepping down from the porch.

Toledo cocked an eyebrow at Sid and rested his palms against the saddle horn. "Just teachin' this smart-aleck kid some manners."

"I see." Sid's eyes turned stormy. He chewed his lip, as if deciding how much truth there was to the new man's words. Levi's reputation for backtalk followed him everywhere. "Light down and haul your stuff inside," he said. He nodded at Andi. "Afternoon, Miss Andi."

Toledo twisted around in the saddle and his expression brightened. "Howdy-do again, miss." He climbed down, doffed his hat, and bowed low. "We haven't been properly introduced. Toledo McGuire at your service." He looked up. "I—"

"This here's Miss Andrea *Carter*," Sid broke in, underscoring her relationship to Toledo's new bosses. "And she ain't got time for idle yappin' with no slicked-up cowhand. She was just leaving." He gave her a look that left no room for argument. "Levi too. They got work to do."

Toledo straightened and settled his hat back on his head. "Well, that's a real shame. It surely is."

Andi felt her face flame. How dare Sid boss her like she was ten years old! And in front of the handsome new hired hand too. She held her ground, fully intending to show Sid he couldn't tell her what to do.

Then she remembered Mitch's advice to mind Sid and Cook and let them fuss. *Help me brush Sid's words off,* she prayed quickly, *before I say something I shouldn't.* She lingered a moment admiring the white stallion then turned to go.

"Sure sorry you can't stick around, Miss Carter," Toledo said. "Sultan would love to make your acquaintance." He slapped his horse's neck. "Wouldn't you, Sultan?"

The horse nickered and tossed his head. His long, black mane rippled.

Andi stepped toward the horse, but Sid's glare kept her from sidling up closer to greet Sultan properly. Beside her, Levi kept a wary eye on Toledo. He looked ready to duck if the new drover decided to pop the knotted rope-end at him again.

Sid motioned them away then rounded on Toledo. "Enough tomfoolery. Get your gear inside if you want a good bunk." He pointed to where the rest of the new hands were headed their way, hauling their saddles across the yard. "It's just for a night or two, but those youngsters will grab 'em quick enough if you don't."

Toledo didn't appear in any hurry to claim the best bunk. He touched the brim of his hat to Andi. "Hope to see you again before the drive."

"Oh, you'll see plenty of us," Andi said. She walked backward to keep Sultan in her sights for as long as she could. "Levi and I are Cook's helpers this trip." Saying it out loud made Andi's heart swell with satisfaction. *I'm really going!*

"You don't say!" Toledo's smile grew wider. "A bright spot to look forward to after a long, dusty day in the saddle. Maybe I'll play and sing for you in the evenings." His hand reached out and rested on a guitar strapped to the bundle tied behind his saddle.

"I reckon you'll be singin' and playin' for the cattle during night duty." Sid's mouth turned down.

Toledo laughed. "That too, old man."

Levi tugged on Andi's sleeve. "Let's go." As they headed back to finish loading the chuck wagon, Andi couldn't miss Sid's words.

"That fella's trouble, and Chad's gonna hear about it from me."

Andi let out a breath. Grumpy old Sid was always quick to find fault with one new man or the other. Sure, Toledo acted a bit too sure of himself, but he was also charming and good-looking. Sid had no call to disapprove of him so openly.

Besides, Andi mused, *I kinda like him . . .*

CHAPTER 6

Getting myself ready for the cattle drive took five minutes. I stuffed a change of clothes and my journal in a gunnysack (I guess I should call it a "war bag" like the cowhands do), rolled up my bedroll, and crammed them both into a nook in the already full chuck wagon.

Mother took me aside and told me to include my toothbrush and tooth powder. She didn't say anything about a hairbrush.

Sunday evening, Chad and Mitch got an earful from their foreman about "that strutting cockerel, Toledo," and his fancy stallion. "What circus did he escape from?" Sid wanted to know. "He's slicker than a snake-oil salesman."

Sid looked downright serious about his concerns. He'd combed his hair and come up to the house to talk with Andi's brothers in the foyer. Hat in hand, the old man groused about Toledo—just like he often let loose his opinion about Andi engaging in ranch activities.

"You oughta send him packing," Sid finished.

Andi paused on her way downstairs. She adjusted her bedroll and her sack of personal items for the drive and listened for her brothers' reply. If Mitch fired Toledo, she hoped he wouldn't do it before she got a closer look at the new man's stallion. And if truth be told, she wanted a chance to listen to the stallion's owner sing and play his guitar.

Chad folded his arms across his chest. "What exactly has he done? Besides going after Levi that one time, which you say you didn't even see." He shrugged. "I haven't heard anything else about it."

Nor will you, Andi thought. Levi had borne his stinging rebuke from Toledo with a stiff upper lip and said nothing to his uncles. Taking his cue, Andi kept quiet too. It was Levi's affair, not hers, especially after he brushed off her concerns with a gruff, "I'm no squealer. I'll work it out myself."

Perhaps Levi realized he'd backtalked once too often and hoped Toledo would let bygones be bygones. *In any case, Levi's not a little boy anymore,* Andi reasoned. He could take care of himself.

"Well"—Sid scratched his whiskers—"Toledo ain't done nothin' I can put my finger on, but he's mighty brash, showing off to your sister and bragging about his guitar. And another thing. His mount don't look like a proper cow pony to me. I just got a feelin'—"

"Listen, Sid," Mitch said, breaking in. "We appreciate your advice and respect your concerns. If he was hiring on to the ranch long-term, we'd let you handle it. After all, you're the foreman. But for this short drive? I can't hire a man one day then fire him the next for no reason. You bring me proof that Toledo's a liability, and I'll send him packing." He paused and looked at Chad for confirmation.

Chad nodded.

When Sid didn't say anything, Mitch continued. "As long as he can do the job, I'm keeping him on."

"Fair enough," said Sid. "You're the boss. Thanks for hearing me out." He slapped his hat back on his head and turned to go. "But don't say I didn't warn you."

The next day, Andi woke just before dawn. A few stars twinkled in the eastern sky when she pulled on a pair of Mitch's outgrown britches, a long-sleeved shirt, and a vest. She splashed chilly water on her face and tightly plaited her thick, dark hair into one long braid. With any luck, it would stay that way for at least a week. Mother would not be along to remind Andi to brush her hair one hundred strokes every night or to comb it fresh each morning.

Andi flipped the braid behind her shoulder and tied a clean bandana around her neck. She put on her denim jacket and jammed her brown, wide-brimmed felt hat on her head. Then she scrambled downstairs. In the hallway, the grandfather clock chimed five times.

"Oh, no!" Andi squealed in alarm. At supper the night before, Mitch had said they'd be long gone before five. "Why did he let me sleep in?" She banged into the kitchen to find Nila and Luisa busy with breakfast. The scent of strong coffee filled the kitchen, as well as the delicious aroma of light, fluffy hotcakes—Luisa's specialty.

"*Siéntate*," the housekeeper ordered when she saw Andi.

Andi hesitated. It looked like everyone else had come and gone already. "But, Luisa, I—"

"*Siéntate.*" Luisa pointed to an empty place at the small kitchen table.

As soon as Andi sat down, Nila bustled over and placed a heaping plate of hotcakes, scrambled eggs, and two sausage patties in front of her. She poured a tumbler of milk and set it beside Andi's plate.

"I can't eat all this," Andi protested weakly. "No time. Mitch and Chad won't—"

"*Tómalo*," Luisa said, coming to stand beside Nila. "It will be your last decent *comida* for many weeks."

The two Mexican women hovered over Andi like mama hawks watching their hatchlings eat every bite. She had no choice but to force the meal into her protesting belly. She was too excited to enjoy it. She washed everything down with hurried swallows of milk and swiped the napkin across her mouth. "*Muchas gracias*, but I've gotta go."

Luisa scowled and shook her head, clearly disapproving of the family's decision to let Andi join the drive. "You will see," she muttered in

Spanish. "After a week of hard, blackened flapjacks, you will wish for the ones you just ate." She shuddered. "You will starve eating such food, *señorita*."

Andi would definitely not starve. She had helped Cook load up the chuck wagon and knew what everyone would enjoy on the trail: beans, bacon, biscuits, and coffee, along with son-of-a-gun stew and apples fried in bacon grease. She and Levi had also hauled lard aboard, as well as flour, sugar, the sourdough keg, and spices of all kinds.

Elizabeth entered the kitchen just as Andi stood up. Levi wasn't with her. "Where's Levi? Did he already eat?"

"Mitch let him sleep in the bunkhouse with the hands to get an early start," her mother replied. "I expect he's out with the herd by now."

Andi's full stomach turned over. It didn't seem fair that Levi—just because he was a boy—got a head start on the trail. She kept quiet, though, for fear her mother might have a last-minute change of heart.

Elizabeth drew Andi into a tight embrace. "Stay safe, sweetheart, and listen to Chad and Mitch." She lowered her voice to a whisper. "You and I are more alike than you might think. When my father died in the gold fields, your grandmother spirited my younger siblings home to Pittsburgh. I stayed behind, reveling in the adventure of the West."

Andi nodded. She knew the story. A warm glow spread to her fingertips. *She understands!* "Don't worry, Mother. I'll do what the boys tell me . . . and Cook too." She had no intention of disobeying her brothers or making herself a pest. The Bakersfield train warning hung over her head like a distant storm cloud threatening rain.

Andi didn't have time to listen to any more instructions or olden-day tales. Worry that she might be left behind spurred her out the back door and down the porch steps. The screen door slammed shut behind her.

"Andi!" Justin dismounted his bay horse and tossed the reins around the corral fence. "Good morning," he greeted her cheerfully.

Andi stopped in her tracks. Her eyes widened. "What are *you* doing here this early in the morning? The sun's barely up."

"I thought a bracing, predawn ride would be just the ticket to start my day."

Andi narrowed her eyes. It looked suspiciously like he'd ridden out to see *her*. What kind of last-minute, big-brother talk did he have in mind?

Justin chuckled at her scowl. "I promised Mother I'd look over some ranch accounts this morning. I thought you'd be long gone by now."

"I was just leaving," Andi said, relieved. "No time to chat. I've got to get out to the herd before the boys sneak away and leave me behind."

"Honey, nobody sneaks a thousand cattle away from *anywhere*. You'll hear them long before you see them."

"Well, then, since I stowed my gear with Cook last night, I'll just saddle Taffy and be on my way. You and Mother have a good visit." She took a step toward the barn.

Justin frowned. "Wait a minute. Didn't Mitch tell you that Taffy stays home?"

"*What?* Mitch knows Taffy and I go everywhere together."

Justin shook his head. "Not on this drive. I'll see to it that Sid turns her out to pasture with Shasta while you're away."

Andi sucked in a breath. "But—"

"You're riding on the chuck wagon with Cook and Levi, remember?" He pointed to the hitching rail, where a homely, dirty-brown horse stood tied up. "It looks like Mitch left you a more suitable horse for a cattle drive. That's your saddle on him, isn't it?"

Andi craned her neck at the horse and groaned. What an ugly beast! "Thanks for nothing, Mitch," she muttered under her breath.

"He probably assumed you'd figure it out when you saw your saddle. You can turn the horse over to the wrangler to keep with the *remuda*."

Andi didn't want to ride that scruffy mount into camp. Worse, once she turned him over to Flint, she'd be afoot, with no horse at all to ride. She opened her mouth to protest, but Justin raised a hand in warning.

"I know just what you're thinking, young lady. Riding up with Cook on the chuck wagon will get old after a day or two. If you think you're going to have your own horse out there and blend in with the others, think again."

Andi scuffed at the dust with her boot toe. *Justin knows me too well.* She *had* considered blending in, but only if the trail boss said so. She'd counted on sweet-talking Mitch into expanding her role as the drive progressed.

"I'm waiting," Justin said pleasantly.

Andi glanced east. The sun had risen over the foothills in a blaze of glory. The herd might be *miles* away by now. She whirled and looked into Justin's face. He wasn't fooling. "All right," she said quickly, itching to be on her way. "I already told Mother I'd mind the boys. I won't go back on my word."

"Excellent news," Justin said in his lawyer voice. "I just wanted to reassure myself that you were clear about your role on this drive as *Cook's helper*." He stressed the words and accompanied Andi to the horse.

Between Mother, Mitch, Chad, and now Justin, Andi's role was clear as glass. "Does he have a name?" she asked, peering at the bony gelding.

Justin slapped him on the rump. "Call him whatever you like."

At the slap, the horse stretched his neck out and snapped at Justin. Justin stepped back.

Andi drew closer. "Dusty," she said, cautiously circling the horse. She stopped when she got in front of his face. "You are Dusty, and there will be no bad manners while we're together. Do you hear me?"

Dusty snorted again, but he pricked his ears forward in obvious interest. He nickered.

"Don't get *too* friendly," Andi warned him. "Just for a few minutes. Then back to the *remuda* you go."

Andi didn't doubt Dusty was a good cow pony. Ornery cows often needed a nip on their rumps to move them along, and Dusty looked mean enough to do it. She wondered why no one had claimed this leftover horse for part of his string.

The instant she mounted, Andi knew why nobody wanted Dusty. He bucked hard and twisted around in a circle. Then he planted his feet and refused to move at all.

"I can't ride this jughead," Andi shouted at Justin. She panted after her nasty scare.

"Sure you can. You just have to work the kinks out of him every now and again." Justin laughed and waved good-bye. "Take care."

Andi fumed. Then she slammed her heels into Dusty's flank. "Move!" He took off like a gunshot. *Boy, can this horse ever run!*

Maybe there was more to mean, ugly Dusty than met the eye.

CHAPTER 7

A cattle drive isn't high adventure, but it sure is fun! We made the first fifteen miles without a twitch of trouble. I had plenty of time between my duties to sit on the chuck wagon's seat and think. With all this grass and plenty of water, the cattle won't lose any weight, and the army will pay their promised forty dollars a head. Forty times a thousand. That's forty thousand dollars— easy pickings. Mitch and Chad will go home very happy . . . and very rich.

Contrary to Andi's fears of being left behind, Mitch had not taken the herd halfway to the King's River without her. Better still, by the time she arrived at the milling cattle, she and her new mount were on speaking terms.

Dusty had tried every trick in the book to dislodge Andi from the saddle, short of bucking her off. He crow-hopped, sidestepped, twisted in circles, and plunged through the foothills at a dead run. He ducked under a few trees to brush her off, but in the end Andi won.

She trotted Dusty into camp. Without even a *buenos días*, Cook told her to get rid of the horse and climb aboard the chuck wagon. "We are heading out," he said, gripping the reins.

Andi was anxious to be free of Dusty too, before anyone else saw her riding him.

Too late. Levi peeked around Cook and snickered. "Where in the world did you dig up that old nag?"

"Where's the *remuda*?" Andi growled. She scowled at Levi. He laughed louder.

"On the other side of the herd somewhere." Cook waved a dismissive hand, silencing Levi. "*¡Apúrate!*" he shouted to hurry Andi along.

Andi turned Dusty toward the small band of horses under Flint's care. It wasn't far. When she slid from the saddle, she noticed Flint eyeing his fifty charges from the back of a sorrel gelding. She uncinched her saddle and let it drop to the ground. "Here's another pony for you," she said, removing Dusty's bridle.

Flint twisted around. His face broke into a smile for Andi, but it quickly turned to a wary frown at the sight of Dusty. He reined his sorrel away, but not before Dusty pinned his ears back and delivered a sharp nip to Flint's leg. Flint yelped.

The wrangler rubbed his leg and glared at Dusty. Dusty snorted. It was clear the two had taken an instant dislike to one another. "Put that outlaw in with the others, would you, Miss Andi?"

When Andi slapped the horse's neck, Dusty joined the *remuda*. Immediately chaos broke out as the dirty-brown horse exerted his leadership.

"He's trouble," Flint muttered. He looked scared. "Give me cattle any day."

"You don't like horses?"

Flint shook his head.

Andi raised her eyebrows in surprise. "Why did you agree to wrangle for Mitch?"

"Miss Andi!" Flint snorted. "For one thing, wrangler goes to the youngest and least experienced." He grinned. "That's me. Another thing. When the boss 'asks' you to wrangle, you wrangle."

Andi took Flint's words to heart. He was wrangling for the same reason she was Cook's helper—because Mitch said so. *I need a little more of Flint's attitude*, she told herself.

"Your brothers pay top dollar, and they don't stint on the grub," Flint went on. "They're good company too—real God-fearing men. I'd be—"

A shrill whinny sent Flint back to work. "Sorry, Miss Andi, I gotta get these ornery critters moving before they scatter clear to the river." He dug his heels into his horse and took out after the *remuda*. To Andi's eyes, it looked like they were scattering already, thanks to Dusty.

"Good luck!" she called after Flint. She hiked up her saddle and lugged it back to the chuck wagon.

"I like cattle drives," Andi announced around the campfire that night. The smell of wood smoke, leather, and strong coffee wafted over her. She shoveled another forkful of biscuits soaked in rich gravy into her mouth and sighed her contentment. "Where else can I get such great chuck?"

Andi liked the food. It was salty and greasy and full of raw flavor. She liked not having to eat with a linen napkin or take dainty swallows of milk. She could gulp hot coffee right along with the cowhands. Better yet, nobody cared if she spilled coffee down the front of her shirt.

Cook grunted his acknowledgment of Andi's compliment and went back to preparing for tomorrow's meals.

"I like 'em too," Levi said. He'd put away twice as much supper as Andi. He sat on the ground between Bryce and Tripp, two of the temporary hands. "I'm not tired in the least."

Chuckles rippled around the campfire. "*Everybody* likes cattle drives the first night out," Wyatt quipped. "You two will change your minds soon enough."

"I bet I won't," Andi challenged.

Mitch grinned. "We'll see." Then he leaned back against his saddle next to Chad. They talked about the route until Toledo brought out his guitar and began strumming. Everyone quieted down, and the trail boss and ramrod joined the rest of the group.

"This song's especially for you, Miss Carter," Toledo said, "since you like cattle drives so much." He broke into a lively tune about the Chisholm Trail. In no time, he had the entire outfit singing along with the last two lines, "Come a ki-yi-yippee-yippee-yi-yippee-yay; Come a ki-yi-yippee-yippee-yay!"

Andi blushed when—on the spot—Toledo made up a verse about how her being along on the drive "will charm the steers right along the trail." His singing made her feel all whirly inside. With an impatient mental wave, she brushed away her silly, confusing thoughts and focused her attention on the merriment.

Left and right, drovers added to the song. Levi came up with a verse about his first-day's mishap at being Cook's helper. He'd tripped carrying an armload of wood and fell head over heels against a pot of beans Cook had set aside. Beans and water flew everywhere. Cook cracked a smile when he heard it. Andi laughed until tears ran down her cheeks.

After Toledo had strummed a dozen songs and everyone's throats were raw from singing, young Bryce cleared his throat. "Have you heard what's lurking in Bear Lake?" he asked in a low, eerie voice.

The hair on the back of Andi's neck stood on end. She glanced around. Twilight had deepened to a dark blue. Stars dusted the sky. Just across the glowing campfire, Bryce sat in the shadows, his face glowing an unnatural orange from the firelight.

Determined not to look like a greenhorn in front of the men, Andi held her peace and didn't answer. But she couldn't help shivering a little.

Mitch chuckled.

Chad elbowed him into silence. "What?" he asked, playing along.

"A serpent ninety feet long," Bryce said.

Andi gasped.

"According to the many who have spied the serpent," Bryce said, "it has a thin head, a large mouth, and small legs that move swiftly through the water." He wiggled his fingers. "It spouts water upwards from its mouth and moves so fast that it leaves a wake behind, much like a boat."

Andi found herself holding her breath. She glanced at Levi, who sat spellbound at Bryce's side, eyes wide.

"Folks have seen the monster crawl up onto the beach with short, flipper-like legs. Once ashore, it holds its head high and turns it from side to side as it looks about." Bryce stretched out his neck and slowly moved it back and forth. Then he raised his hands and grabbed the air. "The Indians inhabiting the area tell stories of how the creature sometimes captures and carries off—"

Something grabbed Andi from behind and wrenched her away from the fire, immersing her in darkness. Terror seized her. She shrieked and clawed to get away. Strong arms held her tight.

"Hey, take it easy!" Chad said. Then he set her free.

Andi crumpled to the ground, too frightened and furious to cry. She shook so hard she couldn't speak.

Chad hung over her, his blue eyes laughing at the success of his prank. He reached down to help Andi to her feet, but she slapped his hand away and found her voice. "If you ever, *ever* s-scare me l-like that again, Chad Carter, I'll . . . I'll . . ." She couldn't think of anything bad enough to do to him. Tears threatened, but her ire kept them back.

"Don't be sore at Chad," Wyatt spoke up, laughing. "The youngest hands always get ribbed. It was either you or Levi, and"—he slapped his knee—"you looked so absorbed in the story that Chad couldn't help himself."

Feeling like a fool and still trembling from the fallout of the Serpent of Bear Lake story, Andi made her way back to the warmth and safety of the fire. She collapsed on a log and buried her burning face in her hands. The men were still tittering. All except Levi. When Andi raised her head she saw him eyeing her with an I'm-glad-that-wasn't-me look.

Andi took deep breaths to steady her pounding heart then looked around. "So," she said, putting on the bravest front she could muster, "what happened to the creature?"

"That, Miss Andi, is a story for another night," Bryce said. "Why, lookee here! It appears it's my turn for night duty." He jumped to his feet and hurried off into the shadows. Laughter followed.

"Well, little sister," Chad said, sliding onto the log beside her. "Do you still like cattle drives?"

Andi thought for a moment. Once her fright wore off, she found herself unable to hold a grudge. "I sure do!"

"Then what do you say I take you out to see the herd? If you think these drovers sing a pretty tune around the campfire, you should hear them serenade the cattle."

Andi knew Chad was exhausted. Why was he being so generous? *He's trying to make up for scaring me,* she thought with a grin. "I'd like that. I haven't seen much from the seat of the chuck wagon. Cook keeps us well ahead of the cattle."

Chad rose. "Find a horse from the *remuda* and meet me just outside camp." He eyed Levi. "You want to tag along?"

Levi shook his head and yawned.

Andi wasn't sure any horse would be eager to let her mount. They'd worked hard today and needed their rest. Creeping up to the chuck wagon, she found a cloth-covered plate and snagged one of the leftover biscuits from supper. Bribery never hurt.

Andi grabbed a spare bridle and hurried to the *remuda*. Peering through the deepening twilight, she spied Sultan's silver-white hide. She ducked under the rope corral and started toward the showy stallion. "Here, boy," she tempted, holding out the biscuit.

Chad had told her to pick a horse. Why not Sultan? She was eager to ride him. Toledo wouldn't mind. *I think he likes me. Why else would he make up that silly verse?*

Sultan seemed happy to nibble the crumbs from Andi's hand, but when she reached out to bridle him, he shied and trotted away. She started after him.

"Andi? You coming?" Chad hollered.

Reluctantly, Andi abandoned the idea of riding Sultan. She grasped the mane of the nearest horse, bridled him, and scrambled up on his bare back. A few minutes later she pulled up beside Chad. Together they rode well away from camp and trotted up a small, grassy knoll.

Andi caught her breath. As far as she could see under the rising moon, inky-black lumps dotted the valley. Above the cattle's lowing, a faint warbling rose into the night air. Three silhouettes on horseback circled the herd and sang back and forth. Andi could almost feel the cattle sighing in contentment.

"Nothing like a good serenading to keep these jumpy critters calm at night." Chad pushed back his hat and nodded his approval at the drovers' careful guarding. "Quite a sight, isn't it?"

Andi nodded, too overwhelmed to speak. It suddenly occurred to her how dangerous a thousand head of cattle could be. A shout . . . a pack of wolves . . . an accidental gunshot . . . any number of things could set in motion a chain of events that would scatter the herd and put everyone in danger.

Only three night guards, she thought. Three guards for a thousand steers. Andi shivered.

CHAPTER 8

I think I spoke a little too soon about the fun and high adventure of a cattle drive.

Mooing . . . bellowing . . . stamping . . .

Andi rolled herself up in her bedroll and drew an extra blanket over her head. It didn't shut out the constant noise of the cattle, but it did keep the mosquitoes away.

For a minute or two.

She heard an annoying whine in her ear and sat up. Heaving the blanket from her head, she slapped at her face. Not quick enough. *That's twenty-one. No, wait. Twenty-two?* Andi moaned. She'd lost count of mosquito bites hours ago.

They had pushed the herd fifty-five miles in four days. Easy miles, Mitch said. He and Chad were in high spirits. The army wanted their beef no later than the tenth of next month, and so far they were right on schedule.

Riding point with Wyatt—one of the Circle C's top hands—Mitch kept the lead steers moving. The rest of the herd stretched out behind in a mile-long column of plodding beef. Flank and swing riders kept a close eye on the stragglers; the drag riders prodded the slowpokes to keep up.

Andi discovered that riding along beside Cook all day might be easy, but the fun of a cattle drive had definitely waned. She endured hours of boredom interrupted several times a day by frenzied scrambling to keep up with Cook's instructions. Worse, her day started during what felt like the middle of the night. It was still pitch dark at four o'clock in the morning.

I'm tired, Andi thought, *but so far it hasn't been too bad—*

A high-pitched whine caught Andi mid-thought. She swatted the mosquito and flopped onto her bedroll near the back wheel. The white top of the chuck wagon showed overhead. *Except for these maddening pests!*

The farther south the outfit traveled, the wetter it grew. At least four rivers and creeks snaked down from the Sierras and met in this part of the valley. The result was a widespread swampy region and lush woodlands before the streams merged into Tulare Lake some thirty-five miles to the southwest.

All day today—riding half a day ahead—Chad had scouted for a dry route around the worst of the wetlands and oak forests. At noon, they'd day-grazed the herd while Andi slapped at mosquitoes and rushed to help Cook fix grub for a dozen hungry men. "It cannot be helped," Cook said when she complained about her bites. "This is the route your brother chose."

By evening, the whining pests grew worse. Andi had worn gloves all day and wrapped a bandana around her face, but to no avail. Her cheeks and forehead were covered with itchy, red bumps.

How can anyone sleep with these greedy bloodsuckers?

Overhead, a gibbous moon glowed high above the oak forest to the east. Andi yawned and focused her sleepy gaze on the campfire a dozen yards away, where a change of night guard was taking place. Three dark forms hunkered down and poured themselves coffee; two others moved off in the direction of the herd, blending into the shadows.

On a whim, Andi rose. Mosquitoes made sleep impossible, so why not go out and listen to the drovers soothe the cattle? Despite Andi's protests, Chad had cut their stay short that first night. A return visit would be just the ticket to take her mind off the biting insects.

Andi flicked a glance at Levi. He lay sprawled under the chuck wagon, snoring softly. *Lucky!* Levi could sleep through anything, even mosquitoes. She crept off to follow the two guards.

Wyatt and Bryce, taking their turn at night duty, had mounted their horses and disappeared like ghosts into a strip of oak forest that edged the camp. She dimly remembered it was a shortcut to the higher ground where the cattle had bedded down.

Andi dogtrotted after the two drovers. The night was cool and pleasant. Moonlight filtered through the trees. Coyotes yipped in the brush, and an owl hooted overhead. Andi's heart raced. *Where did those two cowhands disappear to?* she wondered and picked up her pace.

A root caught Andi's foot and she tripped. *Oof!* She sprang to her feet in alarm and ran, veering around an ancient valley oak covered with wild grape. A willow branch slapped her face. Andi brushed it aside and broke out of the tangled strip of forest.

Finally! Just ahead, the cattle lay spread out in all directions in the clearing. She saw Bryce and Wyatt on their horses and let out a sigh of relief.

"Hey, wait for me," she called in a harsh whisper, fumbling her way over hummocks and dips in the terrain. Andi knew better than to raise her voice and chance spooking the animals. She didn't want to be the cause of any Carter cows stampeding. It would be her last night on the trail if that happened.

"Aw, Miss Andi, it's late," Wyatt chastised her when she caught up. "What are you doing out here? Go back to camp and get some sleep."

Andi looked up at the longtime Circle C cowhand and sighed. "I can't sleep. Not with mosquitoes feasting on me." She cocked her head and listened. "It doesn't sound like the cattle are sleeping well tonight either."

"These skeeters are just like an Egyptian plague," Wyatt said in a disgusted voice. "They can't bite through their thick hides, but they found plenty of ways to make the cattle miserable. All that tender skin around their faces, their exposed eyes." He shook his head. "Poor critters."

Andi shuddered. She knew just how the cattle felt. "They want out of this wetland as much as I do."

"That's a fact," Bryce agreed. "But dust will replace mosquitoes soon enough once we cross the Kaweah." He drew his bandana higher up on his face. "I don't know what's worse."

A deep, soothing voice kept Andi from replying. It would take plenty of sweet-talking and crooning tonight to make these steers forget their suffering. Perhaps the drovers' singing would help Andi forget her misery too.

Wyatt tipped his hat to Andi, and the two men split up and took positions around the herd. Mosquitoes weren't the only creatures that liked to feast on beef. A wolf pack could be lurking, or the most dangerous predator of all—human cattle thieves. Andi was left alone to listen to Toledo McGuire's baritone calming the restless steers.

Toledo and Sultan circled the cattle. He sang slowly, making up the words as he went. When he paused, Wyatt took up the ballad from the other side of the herd, but his voice didn't resonate like Toledo's.

Andi crept closer until she found herself on a rise barely a stone's throw from the edge of the herd. She settled down in the soft grass and clasped her arms around her legs. Then she closed her eyes. Barely breathing, she listened, mesmerized, just like she'd listened when Chad took her out to see the herd. A mosquito whined, but Andi ignored it.

I could listen to Toledo all night long. His singing voice was warm, throaty, and lulling. The cattle responded. Their lowing grew quieter and less distressed. She sighed. *I wish—*

"Good evening, Miss Carter."

Andi gasped and nearly jumped out of her skin. Her eyes flew open. Looming over her not ten feet away, Toledo sat mounted on his fancy rodeo horse. Behind him in the distance, Wyatt and Bryce continued to circle the herd and serenade their charges.

Andi leaped to her feet and stammered, "G-good evening." She brushed loose grass from her jacket and pants.

"It looks like I startled you," Toledo said. "I apologize. I was making my rounds and saw you watching the herd. It was a perfect picture: the silhouette of the cattle settling down under a moonlit sky, the sound of cowpokes singing, and a pretty girl to share it with. Not something you see very often on a cattle drive." He grinned, and his white teeth gleamed in the moonlight. "The pretty girl, I mean."

Andi felt herself redden. Was Toledo making fun of her? Dressed in Mitch's hand-me-downs and with her face a mass of mosquito bites, Andi knew she looked anything *but* pretty. All of a sudden she wished she'd brought along her hairbrush. And maybe worn a split skirt and one of Melinda's lacy shirtwaists instead of her brother's britches.

Too late now. Her tongue felt tied in knots.

Toledo's horse saved the day. He shook his mane and nickered.

Released from the awkwardness of having to speak, Andi closed the distance between them and rubbed Sultan's nose. "He's beautiful," she said. "How does a fine horse like Sultan compare to the others in your string?"

Toledo chuckled. "Sultan outshines them all. You shoulda seen him go after a couple of steers that broke away today. He knows his business. Don't you, Sultan?" He reached down and rubbed the white horse's neck.

Just as quickly, Toledo lost his smile. "Circle C horses are good stock, mind you, but that wrangler you got ain't worth a nickel. He can't control 'em, 'specially the ornery outlaws. He'll get a chunk taken outta his hide one of these days when his back's turned, mark my words. Now, if I was bossing this outfit I'd pull . . ." His voice trailed off when Andi frowned at him. "Pardon my presumption, Miss Carter." He grinned.

Andi didn't return his smile. She knew the *remuda* consisted of good horses, but Flint had a few "Dustys" to contend with too, a job he was not handling well. Every time Andi saw the young wrangler, he was tearing after the scattered horses, constantly rounding them up and trying to keep them together.

But it's none of Toledo's business. None of mine either. "Mitch has it covered," Andi said sharply. She hoped Toledo was wrong about Flint. Surely he and his *remuda* would come to an understanding soon. It had been four whole days.

Toledo made no comment.

Andi rubbed Sultan's nose before turning away. "I only came out to hear you drovers sing for a minute. I better get back to camp before I fall asleep standing up. Cook worked Levi and me pretty hard the last few days, and the nights are too short. If only these mosquitoes would stop pestering me." As if on cue, a mosquito whined. She slapped it away.

"It *is* getting late," Toledo agreed. He cleared his throat. "I can't help noticing how you're admiring Sultan." The horse nudged Andi's shoulder. "I see he's taken with you too. How did you make friends so quickly?"

Andi ducked her head. "I took Sultan a biscuit the first night. He ate it out of my hand. Since then, between chasing down firewood and helping Cook, I've managed to slip away once or twice to bring him a biscuit when he's with the *remuda*." She looked up. "I hope you don't mind."

"Not at all, Miss Carter." Toledo nodded. "Sultan's a sucker for a treat. What do you say he repays you by carrying you back to camp? That way you don't have to walk through the woods or circle around the long way. Never know when you might run into a bobcat or a coyote. These woods are full of 'em."

Prickles raced up and down Andi's arms. How did Toledo know that more than anything she wanted to ride his gorgeous stallion? And she hadn't looked forward to a return trip through that forest on foot. "I'd love to ride him." Her heart fluttered. "And . . . and you can call me Andi."

"Well then, Miss Andi, climb right on up." He reached his hand down and clasped Andi's wrist. Before she could blink, she found herself sitting behind Toledo and clutching his waist. "You settled?" he asked.

"Yes."

Sultan took off at a prancing trot. A cow pony, *prancing*? Andi wanted to giggle. Sultan was clearly more than just an everyday, ordinary working horse. Toledo must have taught him a number of gaits, maybe even—she caught her breath—rodeo stunts. "Do you trick ride?" she asked.

"Sure do," Toledo said. "I do one trick by crawling under Sultan's belly and back into the saddle while he's at a full-out gallop. Another stunt has me flipping over Sultan's head and landing next to him. This fella can stop on a dime."

Sultan trotted through the forest, dodging wild grape and skirting willow saplings, while Andi listened in awe to Toledo's stunt-riding stories. A vision from years ago flashed through her mind: her friend Riley standing on his black horse, Midnight, while the horse loped in a wide circle. Oh, how Andi had wanted to learn that trick! When she'd begged Chad to let her try Riley's stunt, he was firm with his "no." So was Mother.

"I could show you my stunts sometime," Toledo offered. "After the drive, of course. How about when we return to the ranch?"

Andi swallowed. "Maybe." There was nothing she would rather see, but there was little hope of that back on the ranch. Trick stunts were sheer recklessness in Chad's opinion, and his opinion carried weight on the Circle C.

"*Maybe?*" Toledo echoed. He sounded disappointed. "Don't you want to see them?"

"Oh, yes! But Chad wouldn't like it. He says stunts are fine for showing off at a rodeo, but it kills too much of a man's time on a ranch. Not to mention how dangerous it is."

"Your brother sounds like a bit of a killjoy."

Andi jumped to Chad's defense. "He's not really. Our father was killed when his horse threw him during roundup years ago. Chad doesn't like to see reckless stunts around horses. It reminds him of how quickly something can go wrong."

"I'm sorry. I didn't know," Toledo said. "Perhaps you can watch Sultan and me at the Fourth of July rodeo in Visalia instead."

Andi brightened at the idea and nodded. The trip back to camp flew by. Sultan was a fine, surefooted stallion. He picked his way around the worst of the underbrush, even in the faint light. "Do you think I could ride him by myself sometime, Mr. McGuire?" she ventured shyly.

"I don't see why not. So long as you promise to call me Toledo. It would—"

Two men emerged from the shadows near the edge of camp.

"*What in blazes is going on here?*"

Andi's stomach turned a somersault.

CHAPTER 9

There are a lot of unwritten rules on a cattle drive, more than you can shake a stick at. Rules like "obey the trail boss at all times" and "always ride downwind from the chuck wagon so as not to kick up dust." I also know the rule "only a fool argues with a skunk, a mule, or a trail cook." I haven't argued with Cook even once. I do everything he says as quick as I can.

But apparently I missed the rule "never go out to the herd alone at night." I am writing that rule down so I will never forget it.

Silence fell. From the oak forest, Andi heard a coyote howl. More answered, then an owl joined in. From the direction of the campfire, a tin cup clattered to the ground, followed by scuffling noises. The fire popped when someone tossed a chunk of wood in the embers.

Chad stood with his arms crossed over his chest—his usual I'd-like-a-word-with-you expression etched into his dirty face. Andi recognized it even through his four-day stubble.

Mitch was eyeing the two riders with astonishment.

"Well?" Chad's question crackled with anger. He stalked over to the horse and grasped the bridle. "Answer me. What's going on here?"

"I . . ." Andi swallowed, uncertain. Why were they looking at her like she'd done something wrong? "I couldn't sleep, so I went out to see the herd. Like we did the other night," she added quickly. Perhaps Chad had forgotten that earlier trip. How was this any different?

Mitch stepped in and directed his annoyance at Toledo. "You're supposed to be on night guard, mister. Why aren't you at your post?"

"I was escorting the young lady back to camp. What's the problem?"

Chad's smoldering blue eyes told Andi that he didn't like Toledo's cavalier tone. Neither did Mitch, whose usually cheerful features had twisted into a scowl at Toledo's words. Why in the world did they act all tied up in knots when—

In a flash of sudden, overdue insight, Andi's tired mind clicked. She was riding around late at night with a drover she'd met less than a week ago. A rush of warmth crept up her neck and exploded in her cheeks. She was glad for the mosquito bites. The red welts hid her red face.

"The ride's over," Chad said. He held out his hand. "Off the horse. Now."

Suddenly anxious to find her bedroll and escape her brothers' glares, Andi clasped Chad's hand and slid from Sultan's back. He lowered her to the ground then glanced up at the drover. Toledo sat hunched over, leaning his arms against the saddle horn and watching with a sardonic expression.

"Get back to the herd," Chad ordered in a low, tight voice. "I don't want to see your face until your shift ends. If you leave your post again, you're through."

Toledo cocked his head at Mitch. "That go for you too, boss?"

"That's right," Mitch said, planting his fists on his hips. "Chad and I boss this outfit together."

"I see."

Andi bit down on her lip. Could her brothers afford to let a man go this early in the drive? It seemed to her they needed every man—even the inept Flint. Sure, Toledo was cocky, but would they fire him for it? He hadn't done anything wrong . . . or had he?

A minute crawled by. The tension in the air felt thick enough to cut with a knife.

Then Toledo straightened up, gathered his reins, and gave Mitch a two-fingered salute from the brim of his hat. "You're right, boss. I was wrong to leave the herd." He chuckled. "Next time, I'll let your sister wander around in the woods by herself."

"There won't be a next time," Mitch said between clenched teeth.

"I reckon not." Toledo pulled Sultan around and nodded at Andi. "Good night, Miss Andi. It was a pleasure. Let me know when you want to take Sultan for a ride. And I still want to show you those riding stunts sometime, at the rodeo if not sooner." Without waiting for a reply, he nudged his stallion into a trot and disappeared into the forest.

Blood pounded in Andi's ears. Toledo sounded mighty sure of himself. A mosquito droned next to her face but she didn't bother to slap it away. Squaring her shoulders, she faced her brothers.

Chad and Mitch exchanged glances—glances that told Andi nothing. Then Chad shrugged. "You're the trail boss, little brother. I'm hitting the sack. It's close to midnight and I'm beat."

Mitch watched Chad fade into the shadows then gave Andi his full attention. "What in the world were you *thinking*? You're supposed to stay with the chuck wagon and get some sleep. Cook retires every night around nine o'clock. That's your bedtime too, especially when you, Levi, and Cook are up long before the rest of us."

Andi took a deep breath. "I couldn't sleep. The mosquitoes were eating me alive. I didn't think anybody would mind if I went out and listened to the drovers singing to the cattle. Chad and I did it the other night. It's such a lovely, lonely song. The cows settled right down, in spite of all the bugs and mosquitoes."

Mitch seemed at a loss for words. Finally, he sighed. "I don't care if you go out there, Andi. But you're not to go out to the herd *alone*, especially at night. Half these cowhands aren't our own. I don't know them . . ." He paused. "And neither do you."

Mitch had a point. The Circle C ranch hands were loyal and fiercely protective of the Carter women. They'd pulled Andi out of countless scrapes during her life and had earned her family's trust. She could safely follow any of them all over the ranch, no matter how often Sid bellyached about it.

But the new cowhands had not yet earned anything close to trust. "You're right," Andi admitted. Heat returned to her cheeks. "Toledo was just making sure I got back to camp safely." She smiled. "He's really nice, Mitch. He can trick ride and—"

"You stay clear of him, do you hear?"

Andi's stomach lurched. Mitch never snapped at her.

"Sorry, sis," he apologized. "I didn't mean to jump down your throat. I'm tired too." He shook his head. "I don't know what to make of Toledo. He's a superb rider and the best man I've ever seen with cattle for someone his age. But he's an odd fellow. Chad thinks he's a bit of a loose cannon."

The picture of Toledo lashing out at Levi the other day immediately leapt to Andi's mind. "Maybe he is, but I like his horse." She didn't add that she liked Toledo too.

Mitch chuckled. "Of course you do." He draped an arm around Andi's shoulder and led her back to camp. From underneath the chuck wagon, Levi moaned and rolled over in his sleep. "One more thing," Mitch said. "I hate to say it, but if something like this happens again, I won't wait until Bakersfield. I'll send you home from the nearest town. Is that clear?"

Andi nodded, blinking hard. "I'm sorry, Mitch."

Mitch hugged her. "That's good to hear. Just ask next time. Then you won't have to guess. You're doing a fine job for Cook, you know." When Andi crinkled her forehead in confusion, Mitch laughed softly. "He's put aside his grumpiness; haven't you noticed? That means he's accepting your help. And Levi's."

One more hug and Mitch let her go. "We've nearly finished the first week. Think you'll make it the whole way?"

Andi nodded. Relief flooded her that Mitch had taken on the task tonight of dressing her down. Chad would have made a much more thorough job of it, and the evening would have ended in tears and shouting. *Never argue with the trail boss.* She would have broken that unwritten rule for sure if Chad had scolded her.

"I'm glad *you're* the trail boss, Mitch," she said.

"I bet you are." They both knew that when she and Chad lost their tempers, Andi usually came out on the losing end.

"Do you think when you take a turn at night duty, I could come along sometime?" Andi asked, suppressing a yawn. "It's no work to ride around and make sure the cattle stay put. I could guard too and listen to the cowhands sing for three or four hours."

Mitch shook his head. "Not as long as you're working for Cook. The night's short enough for you as it is. I have plenty of men for night duty. Now get to bed."

The lumpy bedroll looked welcoming. Andi collapsed on the ground and rolled up in the extra blanket, suddenly exhausted.

Not even the mosquitoes' whining kept her from drifting off to sleep this time.

CHAPTER 10

One day on a cattle drive is high adventure. Four days is a lifetime. And two weeks? Most likely it will feel like an eternity. The fun is definitely over.

"*Levántate, chica.*" Cook nudged Andi with his boot toe.

Andi's eyes felt gritty. She blinked. The moon had set, but the sun was far from rising. She moaned and rolled over. She was sure she'd been asleep all of five minutes.

Another nudge. "*¡Arriba!* There is much work to be done before dawn."

Feeding more than a dozen hungry men three times a day was not an easy job. Yet Cook managed it well. His bum leg kept him from moving around quickly, but there was nothing wrong with his tongue. He barked orders faster than Andi or Levi could carry them out.

Andi yawned and stretched, then slowly rolled up her bedding. She stashed it in a corner of the wagon, along with the saddle she'd used as a pillow. A wave of dizziness engulfed her. She staggered against the water barrel to catch her balance. She hadn't had a decent night's sleep since they left. Her head pounded. She took a deep breath and turned to face Cook.

A few feet away, Levi sat cross-legged on the ground, hunched over the coffee grinder. Cook had put Levi in charge of keeping the twenty-cup enamelware pot full and boiling hot.

"*¡Ven aquí!*" He waved her over.

Cook's command prodded Andi into action. She brushed the cobwebs from her groggy mind and stumbled to the fire. Day five was not starting well.

Cook furrowed his dark brow. "*¿Qué pasa?*"

"Nothing's wrong." Andi didn't want to give Cook any excuse to criticize her this morning, not after Mitch's scolding last night.

Cook grunted his acceptance of Andi's answer. He cut into a thick slab of bacon and slapped the slices into two large, cast-iron frying pans. Then he handed Andi a long-handled fork. "I'll fry *you* if you burn it," he warned her in Spanish.

"I didn't burn it yesterday," Andi said. *Not much, anyway.* At least nobody complained.

Cook snorted what sounded like a laugh. He shoved his crutch under his arm and shuffled to the back of his wagon, where a large shelf folded down and served as a kitchen counter. Leaning the crutch against the shelf, he pulled out two large mixing bowls and set to work.

Andi bent over the heavy frying pans and turned bacon until her hands started to blister. Hot grease sputtered and jumped out to bite her every time she took out the cooked bacon and set the next batch cooking. "What's Cook talking about?" She sucked on the tender flesh between her thumb and forefinger. "I'm getting fried without his help."

The sizzling bacon set Andi's mouth to watering. Her empty stomach turned over. When Cook ducked around the side of the wagon for a cup of sourdough to add to his biscuit mixture, Andi stabbed a strip of the salty, greasy meat. She held up her fork and blew. Then she popped the slice into her mouth before Cook caught her.

Mmmm! There was nothing like hot, chewy bacon.

As the sky lightened, Andi helped Cook peel and slice a couple dozen apples into the bacon grease and cover the skillets so the fruit could cook down. In the nearby Dutch ovens, the biscuits turned brown and crusty. The coffee pot was nearly boiling over.

Cook banged on the triangle, calling everyone within shouting distance to breakfast. A hoard of sleepy, hungry men milled around the chuck wagon, tin plates and forks in hand.

Chad and Mitch settled down beside the fire and dug into their breakfast. They looked fresh, not at all like men who had spent the last few nights sleeping on the ground. Even Levi looked rested. He spooned up his share of the chow and squatted next to his uncles. A cup of coffee sat next to his feet.

"I like trail drives," Levi announced. "Nobody makes me wash my face or comb my hair or take a bath."

Diego laughed and tousled Levi's hair. "You speak the truth, *chico*."

A few minutes later, the last of the night-duty guards wandered in. So did Flint, bleary-eyed and clearly not ready to face another day with his ornery *remuda*.

Andi knew how Flint felt. She was ready to keel over. The bacon she'd snitched had settled in her stomach in a greasy lump. The biscuits suddenly looked unappetizing, as did the fried apples and strong coffee.

What's wrong with me? Andi wondered, picking at her plate of food. She should be laughing with Levi and shoveling down breakfast like she'd done yesterday. Instead, all she wanted to do was sleep. Or scratch at her face.

Chad spread the map out in front of him and talked with Mitch while he ate. He looked in a hurry to take off on his scouting detail.

I hope he scouts a route far away from this region's pesky insect residents. Andi didn't think she would live through another night like last evening's mosquito attack.

"We'll push south and west for the next few days," Chad told Mitch between mouthfuls of biscuits and bacon. "Soon as we cross the Kaweah and the Tule, we'll have a nice, dry stretch with plenty of grass."

Andi perked up a little at this news. Maybe she'd get a chance to catch her second wind.

Chad took three gulps of coffee and swiped a gloved hand across his face. "After that it's another two or three days to Bakersfield. Then another week south through the mountains and down to Los Angeles."

Mitch nodded. "That's what I was thinking, although it might take longer than we thought to push through the mountains." He poured himself another cup of coffee and sat back for a rare moment of rest. He caught Andi's unfocused gaze from across the campfire. "Seen yourself in the daylight, sis? It looks like you've come down with a bad case of chickenpox. Your face, at least."

Andi jerked fully awake from where she sat leaning against an old log. She smiled wanly. "At last count I think I have twenty-five on my face and neck. They itch like crazy."

"Don't scratch," Cook grunted from the chuck box. "Makes them worse."

Andi didn't need Cook to tell her that. She took a good look at the crew gathered around the morning campfire. Few exhibited bites. The older men all had three or four days' growth on their faces. No mosquito would find a beard easy to poke through.

"Where did you get 'em all?" Levi put down his plate and peered closely at her face. He whistled. "Mosquitoes must really like you."

She frowned. "You have bites too, you know."

Levi laughed. "Bet I don't have as many as you." He glanced around for confirmation.

The men paused in their eating and gave Andi a quick glance.

"Yep, you got a face full, I hafta say," Wyatt said. Long, brown hair hung over his forehead. A full beard protected his face.

"Why do *I* have so many and not Levi?" Andi griped.

"Because you're so sweet," Bryce said, winking at her. "Mosquitoes like the taste of your blood." The other drovers chuckled, and even Andi managed a tiny smile. Next to Flint, Bryce was the drover closest to her age. His own face showed a smattering of bites mixed in with his freckles.

"Time to get moving," Chad broke into the bantering. He rose, finished his coffee, and dumped his plate and cup into the wash basin. "I'm heading out. I'll circle back midmorning when I've found the next site."

Time for me to get to work too, Andi thought. There were dishes to do, the camp site to clean up, and the chuck wagon to pack. Cook liked to keep well ahead of the herd and the *remuda*.

A heaviness overwhelmed Andi. She just wanted to sit still. *A few more minutes*, she told herself. She yawned.

Cook nudged her with his crutch. "Start rinsing the dishes, *chica*," he ordered. "Levi, I am low on wood for the noon meal. Gather more. Once we leave this place, wood will become scarce."

Levi jumped to obey. Andi knew she'd better jump too, but she couldn't make her legs move.

"You all right?" Mitch asked, frowning. He dumped the rest of his coffee onto the fire and peered at Andi.

"I'm fine," Andi insisted. If Mitch thought she was wearing out too fast, he'd send her home quicker than she could blink. She leaped to her feet.

Her world spun. Andi staggered backward, crumpled to the ground, and everything went black.

CHAPTER 11

I've had a minor setback. Too many like this, and I'll find myself on the train home. I must stay strong, no matter what.

"Is she sick?" Mitch's worried voice was the first thing Andi heard when she came around. "She's got enough bites."

Have I come down with the ague? Please, God, no! Not the ague!

Andi dreaded falling ill to marsh fever. She'd seen strong cowhands overcome, lying weak and miserable for days on end with chills, fever, and headaches. When the ague finally passed, the sufferer felt fine for a time. Then just like a sneaky weasel, the fever would attack again without warning. It happened a lot during the spring and early summer—the same time mosquitoes were breeding in the lowlands and around creeks.

Andi opened her eyes a crack. Hovering over her, looking frightened, loomed Cook's dark, wrinkled face. When he saw Andi staring at him, he sat back on his haunches and smiled his relief.

"*Está bien, Señor Mitch.* Her eyes are clear and bright." Cook laid a weathered hand against her forehead. "No fever either." He shook his head. "Besides, it is too soon. Marsh fever does not attack until many days after one travels in the wetlands. There is no need for worry yet." He rose and returned to his wagon.

Andi let out a long, relieved breath and lay still. If Cook didn't think she had marsh fever, then she probably didn't. Cook did more than fix meals on a cattle drive. He was the trail doctor, with cubbyholes in the chuck wagon chock-full of his special remedies. Cook was also expected to act as barber, banker, repairman, and even referee for the occasional spat between cranky drovers.

Andi was happy he'd told Mitch not to worry. She propped herself up on one elbow and smiled. "I think I'm just . . ." She paused. It wouldn't be wise to tell Mitch she was dog-tired. He might put her on the train when they passed Visalia today and send her home. "I stayed up too late last night is all," she amended. "Those pesky mosquitoes. I'll be fine as soon as I catch my second wind."

"We'll see," Mitch said. "I hope so."

Andi accepted her brother's help sitting up. She felt woozy but kept a smile on her face and listened to well-meaning suggestions from the men for a quick recovery. A minute later Cook shooed the well-wishers aside and brought Andi a steaming mixture in an enamel cup.

It didn't smell like coffee. It reeked like one of Cook's home tonics. *Oh, no.*

"*Tómalo,*" he ordered, holding out the mug.

Andi took it and peered into the dark liquid. She took a whiff. Something sweet, strong, and spicy assailed her nostrils. She wrinkled her nose. "What is it?"

"*No importa,*" Cook growled. "*Tómalo.*"

Andi looked up from her cup and into Mitch's face. He nodded.

Warily, Andi took a sip. It was hot, sweet, ginger tea. *Very* sweet. She gagged. "I don't like it," she said, putting the cup down.

"Ginger tea cures dizziness," Cook said with a toothy smile. "I added sugar for extra energy. We have much work to do today. Drink it quickly so there is no delay."

The thought of being the cause of any trail delay spurred Andi into obeying. She closed her eyes, screwed up her face, and gulped the herbal tea down. She shuddered and ordered her stomach not to spew it back up.

Cook grunted his satisfaction. He took her empty cup and set about his work, muttering about having to nurse sick trail hands so early on the drive.

In less than five minutes, Andi started feeling better. She scraped the rest of her breakfast onto her fork and forced it down. Mitch watched her eat every bite. "I'm *much* better now," she assured him and stood up.

Mitch plucked her shirt sleeve. "Now that you can walk without keeling over, I want you to find where the creeks come together and form a little lake. It's a couple hundred yards east in the forest. You can't miss it. Wash up and get back here. You have twenty minutes." He turned to Levi. "Go with her and bring back some wood." He tossed him a rope to tie up a bundle of sticks.

Mitch motioned to Kirby, one of the drag riders. "Give Cook a hand packing up this morning. I don't want to fall behind any more than we already have."

"I'm fine," Andi protested. "I don't need a dunking. I can carry my own weight on this drive. You don't have to ask anybody to do my work—"

Mitch took Andi's shoulders and pulled her close. "Listen to me, *Cook's helper*," he said in a low, soft voice. "When the trail boss gives you an order, you do it quick, and you do it right." He pointed to the line of brush and trees on the eastern horizon, which marked the lowlands. "You get to it, or I'll have my point man pick you up and throw you in."

Andi's eyes grew wide. Mitch meant business, no doubt about it. She peeked around him and saw Wyatt, one of the point men. With Chad off scouting, Wyatt looked ready to step in and carry out Mitch's orders. He grinned at her and waved.

Obey the trail boss at all times.

She gulped. "Sure thing, boss."

"That's better. You now have fifteen minutes." Mitch whirled toward the rest of the milling cowhands. "Show's over. Back to work. Let's move that beef out."

The men scattered. Cook and Kirby piled the dishes and cookware into the chuck wagon, barely scraping things clean. While Kirby packed up the rest of the wagon and put out the fires, Cook worked at hitching up the two horses.

Andi didn't give Mitch another chance to reprimand her. She darted around her brother and past Wyatt. Levi stuck close to her heels, his rope looped around one shoulder and a small hatchet in his hand.

The ginger tea and breakfast had done their work. Andi felt her energy returning. She slowed to a leisurely dogtrot and found the water right where Mitch had said it would be. But it wasn't anything Andi could call a lake. More like a small pond—a dark, still expanse in the early dawn.

"Listen," she told Levi. A few birds chirped. She heard honks and quacks from small waterfowl. Other than that, the water lay quiet, awaiting the new day.

Andi pulled off her boots and socks. She took off her vest and shucked her hat, but that's as far as she went. This was a quick dip, not a real bath. Besides, the thought of soaking her clothes for the coming hot day sounded deliciously cool. Barefoot, she stepped through the thick, dark mud and into the water. "*Brrr!* It's cold. Are you coming in?"

Levi shook his head. "The boss told *you* to wash up. Not me." He grinned. "I'm gonna find some wood." He disappeared into the brush.

Andi looked down. Tiny minnows nibbled at her toes. She waded farther out, then ducked and let the cool water cover her completely. Instantly, her itchy mosquito bites were soothed. "This is more like it," she said when she came up for air.

Sun trickled through the treetops. No time to linger. Andi scrambled out of the pond and back through the squishy mud. Once on high ground, she sat down and scraped off the muck as best she could before pulling on her socks and boots. She stared at her muddy hands. "Wait a minute. Mud's good for mosquito bites."

Before she could talk herself out of it or wonder if the others might laugh, Andi scooped up a handful of dark, slippery mud and smeared a thin layer all over her face—forehead, chin, and cheeks. For good measure, she dabbed a little mud over the half dozen itchy bumps on the back of her neck.

Ah, sweet relief!

Andi washed her hands clean in the shallows, shook them free of water drops, and picked up her hat. She felt one hundred percent better and ready for the day. She made her way through the dense thickets and found Levi whacking at a chunk of deadwood. A growing pile of sticks and large limbs lay at his feet. Andi set about tying them up to drag back.

Levi quit chopping. "What happened to *you?*"

"Never mind." She twisted the rope and secured the knot. "This is probably enough. We'd better head back to the chuck wagon."

Levi didn't answer. Instead, he raised his head and sniffed. "Do you smell that?"

Andi paused. Sure enough, the scent of a campfire drifted in the air. She scanned the woods and saw a thin curl of smoke rising through the trees not far away. *What in the world?*

Overcome by curiosity, Andi nudged Levi and motioned him to follow her. Together they crept closer to the source of the fire and hunkered down just out of sight. What looked like two trail-weary cowhands were scraping their plates and talking. One man had thick, black hair past his shoulders; the other wore a handlebar mustache. Their horses were picketed nearby.

"Just a couple of drifters," Levi whispered to Andi. "Let's go."

"I wonder what they're up to," Andi whispered back.

"Who cares?"

"I think *he* cares." Andi pointed. Across the clearing from the direction of the herd, Toledo McGuire on Sultan was making a beeline for the campsite at the edge of the woods. A chill went through her, and it didn't come from her recent dip in the pond.

Why isn't Toledo with the herd? Why is he meeting up with these two strangers?

CHAPTER 12

My friend Cory says I'm too trusting and ought to be more discerning about folks. Experience has taught me to be a bit more suspicious, but sadly, this often backfires and makes me look like a fool.

Andi's first instinct was to hightail it back to the herd and tell Mitch what Toledo was up to. Visions of cattle thieves and night riders flashed through her mind, one image piling up atop the other. Was Toledo mixed up in this? How could he be?

"Most likely Mitch saw the smoke and sent Toledo back to find out who it is and what's their business," Levi suggested.

A wave of common sense washed over Andi, calming her. Levi had as good a reason as any to be wary of Toledo, yet he showed no suspicion. How would it look if she ran screaming back to camp on a whim? *Just like the boy who cried "wolf" in that old fable.*

Worse, what would Toledo make of her distrust?

Andi flushed. She didn't want Toledo thinking she was a scared ninny who jumped to conclusions. She shook off her misgivings and turned to go. "You're probably right. We better get back before Cook leaves us behind." She hiked up one end of the load of wood; Levi took the rope's other end. Lugging their awkward bundle, they emerged from the oak forest.

In the distance, the chuck wagon's canvas covering looked like a cotton boll against the green-gold rangeland. A dark mass of steers was on the move barely a quarter of a mile behind the wagon. Andi could make out the point men waving their hats above their heads to signal the other riders.

"Oh, *no!*" Andi pulled harder on her share of the wood. "Cook's going to have a fit. You know he likes to stay a mile or two ahead of the herd. Let's *move.*"

Levi was too busy trying to run and breathe to reply. His knees knocked against the bulky load. A hole caught his foot and down he went, face first. Andi tripped and joined him. Both lay panting on the ground.

"C'mon." Andi lurched to her feet and tugged on the rope.

They hadn't gone a dozen steps when pounding hooves caught Andi's attention. She whirled and blanched. Toledo was headed straight for them at a breakneck gallop. Didn't he see them? "Levi! Look out!"

A heartbeat later, the drover did something that made Andi squeal and Levi gasp. Just before he ran them over, Sultan stopped cold. Toledo somersaulted out of the saddle and landed on his feet right next to his stallion's head. The drover hadn't even lost his hat. He touched the brim and said, "Need some help?"

Andi stared at the horse and rider. They stood together as calm as if they were waiting for the morning stage. She gulped and tried to still her hammering heart. She'd never seen such a stunt! No wonder Chad was dead-set against her trying anything like this. It looked deadly.

Next to her, Levi gaped.

"Miss Andi?" Toledo said then he frowned. "Shut your mouth, boy, before you catch a fly."

Levi's jaw snapped shut.

"W-what?" Andi stammered and tried to pull herself together. She wished she hadn't muddied her mosquito bites. She must look a mess. "I mean, yes. We do need help. This load of wood is heavy."

Toledo lifted the bundle with one hand. "I'm happy to tote it back for you." He chuckled. "I thought you might get a kick out of that stunt. If we had time, I could show you a whole slew of them." He glanced over his shoulder. "But I'd best drop this load off with Cook and get back to my post before the boss peels the hide offa me for loafing."

"*Have* you been loafing?" Andi asked. When Toledo cocked an eyebrow, she said, "We saw you passing the time with a couple of drifters in the woods."

Toledo's face clouded for an instant before he grinned. "Nah. For some reason known only to God and your brother, I've been assigned drag duty today. I was stirring up the stragglers at the rear of the line and noticed a plume of smoke. Figured I'd do the boss a favor and see what they were up to."

Andi and Levi exchanged looks. *I told you*, Levi's expression boasted.

Toledo shrugged. "You can't be too careful when it comes to a cattle drive. Those two *hombres* said they're just passing through, headed to Portérville. They'll stay pretty far to the north of us, since they don't want to eat our dust." Toledo's grin returned. "I'll let the boss know." He tied the load of wood around his saddle horn.

"Thank you," Andi said, relieved. *I was silly to worry.* "I hope the wood doesn't chafe against Sultan. It's prickly."

Toledo waved Andi's fears aside and flipped into the saddle, barely touching the stirrups. "He'll be fine." Quicker than Andi could object, Toledo reached down and hiked her up behind him. "So long, boy," he called to Levi and touched his heels to Sultan's flank.

"No!" Andi yelled when she saw Levi dwindling to a dark spot. "I can't leave him behind." But it looked like she could. The only way off Sultan was a long drop to the ground from a galloping horse.

Toledo laughed. "He can hoof it. It's only a few hundred yards, and it'll do the smart-aleck kid some good."

Andi had no time to think up a scathing reply. Toledo pulled Sultan to a bone-rattling stop near the chuck wagon, lifted Andi off the horse, and untied the wood. After a jaunty salute, he spun his horse around and raced off to join the other drag riders.

The camp was deserted except for Cook, who sat on the wagon seat, craning his neck in Andi's direction. *"¡Ándale, ándale!"* He gestured impatiently at her to hurry. His brows drew together. *"¿Dónde está Levi?"*

"He's coming." Andi loosened the bundle and crammed wood into the possum belly. By the time Levi jogged in, she'd thrown the rest of the load wherever she could find a spot and clambered up on the wagon seat. Levi had barely settled next to Cook when the wagon jerked forward.

The chuck wagon lurched and rattled for the next half hour. Hanging utensils and pots clattered against each other. Andi hung on for dear life, exchanging anxious looks with Levi.

"I'm sorry," she told him over the clamor.

He scowled. "Don't worry about it. That ol' Toledo just up and does what he wants."

Andi fell silent. A niggling thought scratched her mind. Mitch had warned her just last night to stay away from Toledo. What would happen if Mitch found out about this latest stunt? Would he send her home? After chewing on it for a stretch, she decided it wasn't her fault and let the matter drop.

The wagon continued to rattle and bounce. Finally, Cook leaned to one side, glanced behind the wagon, and grunted his satisfaction. He eased the horses into a slower pace and relaxed. "Never again will my wagon leave late," he growled. *"¿Comprende?"*

Andi understood, all right. "I won't let you down," she promised. She gave Cook her best smile and picked at the dried mud on her cheek.

He looked Andi up and down without smiling. "If your *mamá* saw you now, *chica*, what would she say?" He slapped the reins to keep the horses moving faster than the cattle.

"My face is that bad?"

"You're a sight," Levi agreed, laughing. "Dripping wet from head to toe, and mud as thick and black as it comes."

Cook shook his head and muttered in Spanish. "I hope this foolishness does not interfere with your work."

"No, sir, it won't." Andi reached behind her shoulder and snagged a pair of gloves. She pulled them on, shivering as an early-morning breeze came up. Her wet clothes stuck to her like a shrunken pair of long johns. "I dare any mosquito to bite me today. I'm refreshed and ready to work hard."

The cool, fresh feeling from Andi's soaking-wet getup lasted less than three hours. The temperature inched higher and higher. Back on the ranch, this weather would be just about perfect. Here, sitting on an open wagon plodding along at a snail's pace under the April sun, it felt like a blacksmith's forge.

Late that morning, the chuck wagon crossed the Kaweah River. Cook allowed Andi and Levi to wade across. The water came a little past Andi's waist. She washed the dried mud from her face and once more felt cool and refreshed.

Out of the soggy lowlands and scattered oak forests, the cattle moved faster. Andi heaved a sigh of relief, but it was short-lived. Dust replaced the mosquitoes. Soon she was gritty and dirty all over. There were no creeks in sight for a quick wash, and the sun blazed hotter than ever.

"You can wash when we camp near the Tule," Cook told Andi that afternoon. "But remember . . . mosquitoes like the shallows." He chuckled.

Andi ignored his odd humor and leaned her head back to rest. She wished she could sleep, but she couldn't afford to keel over the side. She willed herself to stay awake and glanced past Cook's head at Levi. His eyes looked glassy. Cook droned on and on in Spanish, relating stories of his dozens of relatives.

Out of respect for Cook, Andi tried to pay attention. The longer she listened, though, the more his words buzzed in her ears. She finally tuned him out.

The next few days blurred together into a monotonous routine. When Cook stopped the chuck wagon in a grassy area and set up for supper,

Andi went through the motions of helping. She started the fires and set up the tripods for the large pot of stew Cook had begun to prepare the night before. Levi found firewood and endlessly refilled the water barrel. Then he settled down to grind coffee beans.

Beans, bacon, and biscuits. *More* beans, bacon, and biscuits. A dab of stew. An occasional plate of flapjacks and molasses. A pan of fried apples. Gallons of coffee. Did these men do nothing but eat, sleep, and prod cattle? Andi felt she did nothing but cook and wash dishes. *Why did I ever want to come along on a cattle drive? I feel like a kitchen maid.*

Never in her life had Andi been so dirty, tired, and snappish. She was tired of the food, tired of the bellowing cattle, tired of the hard, dusty ground. And tired of riding on a chuck wagon that seemed to move slower than a turtle. But most of all she was tired of being *tired.*

Her only diversion came when—between wiping dishes and straightening up—she listened to the cowhands tell stories around the campfire. At least when she could stay awake long enough.

"This ain't no made-up story," Bryce insisted when Toledo snorted at one of the young drover's more outrageous tales. "My great-uncle Jack served at Fort Tejon back in '58 and saw those camels with his very own eyes. They were packing supplies down to Los Angeles."

Andi's eyes opened wide; her sleepiness vanished. She sooner believed Bryce's tale about the sea monster in Bear Lake than this cock-and-bull story about camels in California. Toledo was right to snort his disbelief.

"If they're so doggone real, then where are those camels now?" Seth, one of the temporary hands, demanded.

Bryce shrugged. "Heard tell the Apaches had a hankering for camel steaks." Laughter rippled through the group. "The soldiers hated those beasts with a passion. Uncle Jack said one lone camel was meaner than a whole herd of army mules. The government finally gave up and let 'em loose."

"Aw, you and your uncle are tetched in the head," Wyatt scoffed. He dumped the remains of his coffee in the fire. "I've heard enough fanciful tales. I'm for bed."

Andi had not heard enough. Her eyelids drooped, but she couldn't help asking, "Are there any camels left, or did the Indians eat them all?"

Bryce turned his smiling, freckled face to Andi. "Well, Miss Andi, what camels didn't get killed just sort of wandered off, some into the Mojave Desert, where"—he lowered his voice to a whisper—"they are to this day."

"You're foolin'!" Levi burst out.

"I ain't. Might even be a few camels still moseying around the old fort grounds. But they're hard to catch a glimpse of." He nodded soberly. "Might get a chance of seeing one, though, if you're stealthy enough."

Toledo laughed. "Sounds to me like you're aimin' to send the kid on a snipe hunt." He rose and left.

"What's a snipe hunt?" Levi asked.

Andi bent close to his ear. "It's like a wild-goose chase," she whispered. "It means there aren't really any camels at the fort, so don't waste your time looking for them."

Levi glared at Bryce.

Andi rolled up in her blanket that night and shivered, in spite of the warm, spring evening. Their route would take them straight through the old Fort Tejon grounds, which were now part of a huge ranch. Might there really be camels there?

Of course not! But Andi fell asleep with visions of humped, Arabian camels parading around in her dreams.

CHAPTER 13

I have come to the conclusion that Mother and the boys already knew what I have only just figured out: I am a greenhorn when it comes to riding the trail. I can't wait to see Los Angeles and sink my teeth into a thick, juicy steak. I'm also looking forward to exchanging my bedroll for a feather bed and Mitch's britches for a pretty dress. I have had more than enough of trail life.

Good thing Mitch is not a snoop. If he read this journal entry he would send me home. And I am not a quitter. A Carter never gives up.

"The drive gets easier from here on out, right?" Andi asked Cook at the beginning of another long day's ride. "We're almost to Bakersfield—through the worst of it, right? All that dust . . . and those horrid mosquitoes and soggy lowlands." She took a deep breath and hoped the old Mexican would confirm her words.

Last night Andi had battled with herself over the possibility of a Carter admitting she was ready to go home; this morning she'd taken a deep breath and decided she would stick it out to the end. For one thing, there was no chance she'd let Levi finish something she couldn't finish. And Levi looked like he had no intention of quitting. *I wish he'd spare me some of his energy*, Andi thought.

Cook gave Andi a sidelong look. "*Chica*, there is no easy part of a cattle drive."

Andi's stomach knotted. Was he kidding? She looked into his black, deep-set eyes for an indication that he was pulling her leg. Dead seriousness held her gaze until Andi looked away.

"The Tehachapi Mountains are a steep climb," Cook went on. "The weather is growing hotter. The cattle will become restless. The men will tire." He shook his head and sighed. "We still have a long way to go."

Andi bit her lip and straightened her shoulders. *I can do this! I have to!*

Midmorning, Chad returned from his scouting detail looking grim. He reined his horse to a slow trot alongside the chuck wagon and said, "We've got a problem."

Chad's ominous words were meant for Cook's ears, but Andi brushed away her sluggishness to listen. She exchanged a worried glance with Levi. What could possibly go wrong now?

"*¿Sí, señor?*" Cook kept the horses at a steady, clopping pace.

"The Kern is running unusually high."

Silence from Cook. "A storm upriver?" he finally asked.

Chad shook his head. "I'd guess the snowpack's melting faster than we expected for this time of year."

Cook's look darkened and his fingers tightened around the reins. "We will chance such a crossing, *señor*?"

"We don't have a choice," Chad said. "I say we cross while we can. Right now it's doable, but that could change in a heartbeat."

Cook grunted. "Perhaps you are right. I have seen the Kern in full flood, when it overflows its banks clear to Bakersfield."

Chad nodded. "It's nowhere near to flooding, or I wouldn't even consider it. A good thing too. We'd be stuck with a thousand head of cattle and no way to get them to Los Angeles."

That would end our cattle drive real quick, Andi mused.

"It must be done," Cook muttered, "*pero no me gusta*." He shook his head.

"I don't like it either," Chad said.

Cook brought the chuck wagon to a stop and regarded Chad with a scowl. "Everyone is tired, and the cattle are balky. They will not want to cross such high water."

"I know." Chad settled his gaze on Andi and Levi. "You two stick close to Cook for this crossing."

Andi's jaw dropped. "But *why*? I've forded all the other rivers with no mishaps."

Crossing the rivers and the innumerable valley creeks had become Andi's favorite part of this dull cattle drive. She and Levi splashed through each one and came out soaking wet and refreshed. It was high adventure, especially when a river turned deep and Dusty had to swim.

Andi had her heart set on fording the Kern and enjoying another cool dip. "How high can it be, anyway?"

"High enough," Chad snapped. He looked in no mood for an argument. "Just do as you're told."

Andi's promise to mind her brothers flew right out of her head. She could take care of herself much better on the back of a horse than on the floating chuck wagon. Angry words flew from her mouth before she could stop them. "You're not the trail boss. I'm going to ask Mitch."

"*Silencio, chica,*" Cook broke in before Chad could react. "You work for *me*, so listen well. You and the boy will not be allowed to cross this river on horseback as you have done before. You will ride with me."

Andi gulped. Now she'd done it—stuck her foot in her mouth in front of Cook.

Chad laughed and touched the brim of his hat in salute. "*Gracias,* Cook. I couldn't have said it better myself." Then he turned serious. "I want you to drive the wagon ahead and find the best place for taking it across. Then rustle up some grub for the men as quick as you can and get ready to cross. After that, we'll move the herd several hundred yards downstream to cross, well out of your way."

"*Sí, señor.*"

Chad removed his hat, wiped a sleeve across his sweaty brow, and plopped it back down. "We can't afford any delays." He spurred his horse toward the front of the herd, where Mitch was riding point with Diego.

As soon as Chad galloped away, Cook slapped the horses into a fast trot. The chuck wagon lurched and bounced over the rough ground; Andi lurched and bounced all over the seat. "You drive this wagon like we're trying to outrun a thunderstorm." She gritted her teeth. "What's the rush?"

"You heard your brother. We will cross the river soon. Everything must be secured aboard the wagon, and there is a meal to fix. We have much work to do before the rest of the outfit arrives."

For the next hour Andi rode silently next to Cook and held on while the wagon jolted closer to the riverbank. Levi followed suit. How dull it would be to float across the Kern River on a chuck wagon while everybody else was fording it on horseback! Worse, staying aboard the wagon kept Andi from getting wet and cooling off. Already she felt hot, gritty, and sweaty.

Why can't Levi and I ride across?

The answer became clear when Cook slowed the wagon to a stop on a wide, flat rise above the river. He stood up from his seat and scanned the riverbank in both directions. Then he mumbled something too low for Andi to catch, sat down, and urged the horses upriver.

While Cook looked for a suitable crossing point, Andi watched the river. It stretched from east to west in a broad, fast-moving current. She didn't know how deep or wide this body of water flowed on a normal spring day, but right now it looked mighty high. Whole, leafy branches bobbed and twisted on the surface as debris floated downriver. Thick vegetation lined both banks.

Andi couldn't see any good crossing place.

"Get busy," Cook shouted.

Andi jumped. Cook had stopped the chuck wagon on a wide clearing about fifty feet from the water. The opposite bank appeared welcoming and free of undergrowth.

Cook rattled instructions at lightning speed, nearly shoving Levi off the high seat in his hurry to begin preparations. Andi hopped down and lent a hand, securing supplies so they wouldn't float away.

Levi saved enough water for the noon coffee then emptied the fifty-gallon water barrel attached to the wagon's side to lighten the load. He tossed every stick of wood from the possum belly to the ground.

"What we do not use now, we will leave," Cook said. "You can gather more after the crossing."

Levi groaned. It was a beautiful pile of firewood. "I hate leaving it behind," he grumbled.

Cook ignored him and grabbed a piece of the canvas cover. He tied it down tighter.

When the last supply had been stowed according to Cook's exacting standards, he wiped his hands on his wrinkled, once-white apron and said, "Now, for the grub. Biscuits and gravy—maybe a little salt pork—just enough nourishment for the men to get those balky steers across."

It was past noon by the time the herd drew near. Andi heard the cattle before she saw them. Lowing and mooing, they were bunched together about a quarter mile downriver and set to day-graze while the men took turns eating.

The drovers wolfed down their food, but none forgot to compliment Cook. "I'm stacked to the fill," Wyatt said, patting his belly. The others agreed. Andi didn't see how it could be true. It seemed like a skimpy meal to her. Cook gave the hands a toothy smile, promising better chuck at the next stop.

In no time, the camp took on a feeling of frenzied activity. Mitch shouted orders and Chad took off for the herd. When Mitch brushed by the chuck wagon, Andi saw her chance to appeal to him about fording the river.

"Mitch!" She snatched his sleeve as he passed.

He paused. "Make it quick. I need to head out."

Andi opened her mouth to plead her case. Cook stood a dozen feet away, wiping his hands on his apron and watching her. One dark eyebrow rose, and he shook his head.

"I . . ." She faltered. It suddenly dawned on her that Chad could be right about this river crossing. It already felt different from the others. The men seemed nervous, trying to cover it with loud talking and running around.

It might really be dangerous, she thought. Cattle could be swept downstream; horses might panic and dump their riders midstream. Even her brothers, who seemed so strong and confident, could be hurt.

Her desire to ford the Kern River on horseback vanished.

"Don't look so glum, sis," Mitch said. He pulled his gloves on and grinned. "Most of us have crossed higher water than this before. Just stay with Cook and do what he says, all right?"

Andi nodded. Mustering a shaky smile, she stood on tiptoe and planted a quick kiss on Mitch's cheek. "Be careful."

"You too." Mitch tweaked her nose. Then he was gone, along with the entire crew, to prod a thousand ornery cattle into the cold, deep, swift-running water.

Keep them safe, God, Andi prayed and went back to work.

Cook scrubbed while Andi and Levi wiped dishes as fast as they could. As soon as the pots and pans and utensils were safely stowed, Cook closed up the chuck wagon and climbed aboard. "*Vámonos*," he ordered.

Time to go.

Levi clambered up one side of the wagon and Andi climbed up the other side. Cook took the reins and urged the horses forward. The wagon jolted and bumped its way down the bank and into the river. The horses seemed eager to get the crossing over with and didn't slow their steps, not even when the river reached their bellies. They just snorted and kept moving.

"This isn't too bad," Levi said. But his face was pale and he clutched the wagon seat with both hands. The horses plunged onward.

Just then solid ground dropped away. Andi's stomach leaped to her throat. She gasped. The wagon was floating. Cook sat calmly and yelled encouragement to the swimming horses. They splashed for the opposite bank but were not strong enough to fight the current. The wagon slowly began to edge its way downriver.

Andi grasped the wooden supports tighter. The river looked deep. And frightening. The current flowed swifter out here in the middle, and it was a long way to the other shore. A sense of helplessness washed over her. She closed her eyes and prayed, *I want off! Please, God, make the horses go faster.*

Thunk!

Andi's eyes flew open at the jolt. Levi yelped and nearly tumbled off his seat. With one hand, Cook yanked him upright and steadied him. His other hand gripped the reins. "It is only a little debris from upriver. *No se preocupe.*" He set his jaw and tightened his hold on the horses.

Don't worry? What kind of advice was that? Andi felt plenty worried, especially when she saw a second snag headed their way. She pointed a shaky finger. "Look! Another one."

"Hold on!" Cook yelled.

Whack! The impact near the back end sent the wagon into a slow, lazy spin.

The horses thrashed and tried to turn for shore, but it was no use. The chuck wagon drifted downstream, out of control and headed straight for the wall of cattle. What would happen when it reached the mass of swimming, bellowing bovines?

Andi shook with terror. She didn't want to find out. "C-Cook," she stuttered. "W-what—"

Splash! Cook plunged into the river and came up swimming. He looked at home in the water, even with his bad leg. His strong strokes made short work of the distance to the horses' heads. When he found a bridle, both animals settled down and let Cook lead them toward the south bank. Their thrashing hooves began to make progress.

Andi's pounding heart returned to normal. They weren't out of the woods yet, but Cook had control of the situation. Andi slid across the seat. She caught Levi's hand and gave it a reassuring squeeze. "We're almost there. Cook's working wonders with those horses. Hang on a little—"

Without warning, another chunk of debris struck the wagon dead-on. Andi heard a *crack*, and the wagon listed, sending her and Levi plummeting over the side and into the river.

CHAPTER 14

We left the easy part of the drive behind us the minute the horses stepped into the Kern River.

Andi broke the surface of the water and gasped. She could swim a little, but this was not her idea of a summertime splash in the creek. The Kern River didn't batter and toss her around like the storm-choked, muddy and churning Dry Creek had done a few years ago, but she knew it was just as dangerous . . . and it was so *cold!*

An arm's length away, Levi's head popped up. Gagging and flailing, he took a breath, bellowed his terror, then disappeared under the current. Instantly, Andi gripped his shirt and held on tight. He came up for air. "I can't swim!"

"Don't fight it!" Andi yelled back. "I've got you. Just keep your head up and try to float." A mouthful of river water made her sputter. "Stop splashing!"

Levi panicked, ignoring Andi's advice. He tried to rip away from her tight hold. He kicked and splashed harder. When he went under again, he dragged Andi down with him. Dark, chilly water filled her eyes, her nose, and her mouth, but she didn't let go.

If I let go, Levi will drown. The possibility flashed through her mind with appalling clarity. *But if I don't let go, we might both drown.*

Desperation energized Andi's legs. She held her breath and kicked her way to the surface. She sucked in air and blinked to clear the water from her eyes. When she could see again, a new terror struck. The herd! The river was carrying them straight for the cattle.

Andi looked around wildly then struck out swimming for the nearest shore. She forced her limbs to obey; her free arm plowed through the water, but she made no progress. Levi's flailing kept them stuck in the middle of the current, while the river continued to pull them farther downstream.

Panic set in. Andi's heart pounded and her ears felt full of water. Where were Cook and the wagon? Had he seen them fall in? Did *anyone* know they were missing? Probably not. Mitch and Chad had their hands full bringing the balky cattle and the *remuda* safely to the other side of the river.

A leafy willow branch floated by, reminding Andi how she and Levi had plunged into the river in the first place. If another big chunk of wood slammed into them, it could be the end of them. She thrashed harder and hauled Levi up for another breath of air. Doing so thrust her underwater once more.

I can't keep doing this, Andi realized the next time she took a breath of sweet air. She already felt winded, as if she'd run a mile and a half without stopping. Her teeth chattered. Worse, they were closing the distance to the herd. Andi could see the animals now. They looked like the miniature wooden steers she used to line up when she was little, to play she was going on a cattle drive.

That dream is shattered.

A choking, gurgling sound from Levi tore at Andi's heart. Her nephew was drowning, no matter how hard she tried to keep him afloat. If only there was something to grab on to—a chunk of wood, a log, a—

There! Two or three strokes away, a large cottonwood limb drifted along beside her. Andi mustered enough strength to reach it. Just as it floated past, she lunged and curled her fingers around the leafy tops. Another jerk and the branch came closer. It took all her strength to hang on to it.

Hurry, hurry! The cattle were closer now and looked a lot bigger. Over the splashing river current, she could hear their frantic bellowing. She heard shouting too, and the high-pitched screams of terrified horses. Like Andi, the animals swam for all they were worth, but they were slowly being dragged downriver.

Andi inched her fingers along the cottonwood debris and discovered it was a large branch—round and solid enough to hold Levi up so she could concentrate on kicking to shore. She took a deep breath and heaved him into the mass of branches. He stopped struggling and lay across the brushy raft with his eyes closed, making gagging sounds.

At least he's still alive and his head's out of water.

To Andi's relief, she found the driftwood easy to guide. She grabbed the limb with both hands and forced her legs into a churning frenzy. Slowly but surely she pushed her precious cargo toward the south bank. When her feet touched bottom, she burst into grateful sobs. She slammed the cottonwood raft into the sloping riverbank, leaned over Levi, and closed her eyes. *Thank You, God!*

Andi felt as if she'd just swum the mighty Mississippi River.

Before the Kern could snatch its victims back, Andi staggered out of the water and crumpled onto the bank next to Levi. She gasped for breath, choking and sobbing and shaking. "This c-cattle drive is g-getting worse and worse," she stammered between chattering teeth.

Levi didn't answer. He lay on his belly in the midst of the leafy river debris. Seeing his still form, Andi caught her breath. *He can't be dead. He can't!* How would she ever face Kate if Levi drowned? *Please don't let him be dead*, she prayed.

She forgot her own fatigue and squatted beside her nephew. "Levi!" She shook him hard. "We're safe. We made it. Wake up."

Levi groaned. Then he drew a ragged breath and started coughing. Water dribbled past his bluish lips just before a good portion of the Kern River spewed from his mouth. He moaned and opened his eyes.

Andi helped him roll over to sit up. She hugged him and started crying again. "Oh, Levi, I was so scared you might have drowned!"

"Hey," Levi said, batting weakly at her attempts to comfort him. "No mushy stuff." He coughed again, loud and deep.

Andi laughed and let him go. "Sorry." She brushed her soaked sleeve across her eyes.

Side by side, the two sat on the muddy, vegetation-choked riverbank, drained of energy. Andi stared at the river, watching the current flow by, glad she was no longer a part of it. A deep shudder went through her. Tears pricked her eyes once more. *It's over*, she told herself. *No need to blubber. We're safe, thanks to God's grace and a cottonwood branch.*

Andi knew she should get up. Cook was probably ashore by now. She could imagine his dismay over losing his passengers. What would Cook tell the Carter brothers if he'd lost their sister and their nephew? "We better let Cook know we're alive," she mumbled.

"Uh-huh," Levi agreed. He didn't move.

Andi couldn't move either.

It's over, she told herself. Her head lolled forward and she dozed.

Andi woke to the sound of drumming hooves, yelling cowhands, and a loud bellow. "No, *no!* Let 'em scatter!"

Astonished, Andi realized that when need be, Mitch could holler just as loudly as Chad. He was yelling now, and nobody within a hundred yards could miss his words. His throat was surely throbbing. "If you don't, they'll stomp each other sure as we're drenched!"

A pause, then Mitch's voice rose higher. "I said *let them scatter!* We'll round 'em up later when they calm down."

Andi dragged herself to the top of the riverbank and peeked around the trunk of a large willow tree. Her heart slammed against her rib cage. Less than twenty-five yards away, Mitch was riding hard and fast, cutting close to a writhing mass of cattle gone berserk. Their horns slashed at each other as they stampeded in order to find a way out of the confusion.

The cows raced for freedom, but they didn't seem to know which way to go. They ran in a trampling swarm of hooves and horns, smashing into each other and bawling their terror. One big fellow broke loose and plowed across Mitch's path. His horse reared and veered out of the way just as the crazed steer tossed his horns. Mitch narrowly missed being gored.

Horror seized Andi when his horse stumbled and tipped sideways. "No!" she screamed, but Mitch couldn't hear her above the clamor. He stayed in the saddle and maneuvered his horse to regain its footing. Then he galloped away. "Oh, be careful, Mitch!" She buried her head.

Andi looked up when she heard a new sound. Mixed in with the frantic herd were a number of terrified horses. They reared and whinnied, searching for a way out of the whirlwind of bovines. Their screams only stirred up the cattle and bewildered them even more.

Cowhands surrounded the herd at what Andi hoped was a safe distance. Apparently, not safe enough. Mitch swerved and shouted again, waving the drovers off. Saving lives—the men's and the cattle's—clearly remained his top priority. They could assess the damage later.

Chad was nowhere in sight.

Levi crawled up beside Andi. "What's going on?" he asked sleepily.

"The herd's stampeding," she said in a tight voice. "It also looks like Flint lost control of the *remuda* crossing the river. It's a dreadful mess. By the time it's over, those cows and horses will be scattered from here to Bakersfield."

Andi trembled. The thought of a stampede froze her to her bones. If something as trivial as a sudden, unfamiliar night sound could set the cattle off, it was little wonder this risky river crossing—combined with Flint's inept handling of the horses—caused the herd to bolt in bellowing chaos.

The cattle had dwindled to a running mass of black dots before Andi felt like standing up. She shaded her eyes, looked around, and sighed. Bunching those steers would most likely take the drovers the rest of the day. Rounding up the frightened *remuda* would probably take longer, since young Flint could hardly manage it on his own.

"If I had a horse, I could help," Andi said.

"What?" Levi rose beside her. "What are you talking about?"

"The men are off chasing down cattle. Probably no one's thought about the horses, but if Flint can't corral them, we'll be awful shorthanded. It doesn't look like anyone's spared a second to find out what happened to you and me. We'd best go show Cook we're all right."

Andi sat down and pulled off her boots. Water streamed from them. Then she jammed her soaked feet back in, stood, and waited for Levi to do the same. "Hurry up," she said.

Circling the underbrush, Andi jogged east along the riverbank, with Levi at her heels. A few hundred yards upriver, a disheartening sight met her eyes. The chuck wagon sat lodged in river mud, the horses straining to pull it up the embankment. From behind the wagon, Toledo and another cowhand, Tripp, jabbed and poked at the half-sunk back wheels. Mud flew in all directions. So did the rough language.

Andi drew closer. Cook was tugging at the horses' bridles, coaxing the animals in a mixture of English and Spanish. "Cook!" she hollered and waved.

"*¡Gracias a Diós!*" Cook shouted when he saw Andi and Levi running toward him. "You and the boy were not drowned in the river as I feared. I dreaded having to tell the *señores* such news, on top of everything else." He smiled. "Now they will be spared this grief."

If the old Mexican felt anything more for his young charges, he hid it well. "Get busy," he barked, "but stay away from this." He jerked his chin toward the wagon. "It is a dangerous business."

"What if Levi puts together some kind of rope corral while I help Flint bring the *remuda* back?" Andi suggested. Tired as she was, she knew Mitch would need every spare hand to pitch in and salvage what livestock they could. She refused to find petty make-work or sit around and twiddle her thumbs while the entire outfit roiled in turmoil.

Cook required no convincing. *"Sí, sí,"* he agreed eagerly. "There is little doubt the wrangler needs help. He raced by here not long ago, white-faced and desperate to round up those ponies." He waved a hand in the general direction Flint had gone. "Find a horse and don't come back without the *remuda.*"

CHAPTER 15

Things have gone from bad to worse since crossing the river. Every time I try to record what happened, my eyes tear up and my fingers shake. I never counted on this kind of "adventure."

With Cook's approval, Andi made plans. Levi would construct the holding pen for the horses; she and Flint would bring them back. That way the rest of the men could concentrate on rounding up the scattered herd and quieting them before dark. She smiled to herself. Wouldn't Mitch be pleased to find the scattered horses corralled and fed when he and his weary men returned from their own tasks!

But in order to go after the stray horses, Andi needed a horse of her own. Every spare mount already held a rider, and the extra horses in the *remuda* were scattered as far and wide as the cattle.

Except for two.

Andi saw a flicker of movement in the brush lining the riverbank, a stone's throw from Cook and the cowhands digging out the chuck wagon. She hurried over and found Toledo's horse ground-tied and foraging along the bank. Tripp had left his horse grazing too.

Sultan lifted his head and nickered when Andi approached.

"Howdy, Sultan," she greeted him. "How would you like to take a little ride?" Without waiting for an answering whinny or asking Toledo, she hiked herself up in the stirrups and settled comfortably into the saddle on the magnificent stallion's back. She fingered the catch rope, just in case she needed to lasso a skittish pony.

Like that jughead Dusty.

"This is going to be pure pleasure." All weariness fled as Andi set her mind on the coming task. She thought she heard a muffled "Hey!" from the chuck wagon, but she nudged her mount without turning around. Time was of the essence, and hadn't Toledo told her she could ride his horse sometime?

Now is a good time, Andi reasoned. Sultan bounded into a lope at the slightest command.

A half hour passed before Andi saw Flint in the distance. He'd cornered about two dozen horses in the delta region south of Bakersfield. She groaned. More swamps. Splashing through the wetlands and dodging willows, she hailed the wrangler. He lifted his hat and waved it vigorously.

Andi wished she could wave back, but she'd lost her hat in the river. The sun glared in her face, forcing her to squint to see what Flint was up to. "Yoo-hoo!" she called. "Need a hand?"

Flint motioned her over. "I'm sure glad to see *you*," he said when Andi reined in beside him. The bandana wrapped around his forehead was grimy and bloodied. He sighed, replacing his filthy hat. "Didn't do so good at the crossing," he confessed sheepishly. "One minute I was drivin' those ornery nags across; the next minute I woke up in the mud with a headache. Been scramblin' after 'em ever since." He looked worried. "Reckon your brother'll fire me?"

Andi shook her head. "Not if we bring them in before Mitch gets back with the cattle. Levi's working on a rope corral." She nodded toward the partial herd, which grazed in the plentiful marsh grass. "Let's get these back and then we'll go after the rest."

Flint grinned his agreement and they took off.

It didn't take Andi as long as she expected to coax the horses to leave the wetlands and all that rich fodder. Sultan proved he was more than just a show-off rodeo horse. He lit into the stubborn *remuda* with hardly any urging from Andi and led them back to camp. All Andi had to do was stay in the saddle. Flint trailed behind the group to keep the nervous horses from bolting.

"That's half the batch," Flint said when Levi had secured them inside the makeshift corral. His wide smile showed Andi his gratitude. "But the rest might not cooperate so easy."

"We'll split up and drive them back one by one if we have to," Andi said, loosening her catch rope.

They didn't have to. With sweaty flanks and quivering muscles, the rest of the scattered *remuda* seemed happy to return to the familiarity of the trail-drive corral. Andi was forced to lasso only the ornery Dusty, and it took her three tries. He could dodge quicker than a jackrabbit. But so could Sultan, and in the end Dusty trailed behind Andi and Sultan like a puppy on a leash.

"Are you sure that's all of them?" Levi asked when he secured the corral rope around the trunk of a small valley oak. "I've been counting as they come in, and I come up short."

Andi and Flint dismounted and exchanged anxious looks. Each knew what the other was thinking. *Are the other horses simply out of sight or were they trampled in the river chaos?* Neither spoke their worries aloud.

A loud, angry, "Hey, there!" made Andi spin around. With mud caking his trousers up to his knees, Toledo stalked across the clearing. His eyes blazed in his sunburned, clean-shaven face. Not far behind, Cook sat on the now-freed chuck wagon, driving it toward the temporary corral. Tripp was gone, most likely lending Mitch an extra hand with the herd.

It took Andi only the blink of an eye to realize who Toledo was yelling at. He barreled down on her and stopped less than a foot away. "You took my horse without a by-your-leave and made a mess of him!" His gaze swept over the mud-splattered legs of the white horse, and he swore.

Andi stumbled backward as if struck. Her ears burned, and so did her cheeks.

"Hey!" Flint jumped in. "Watch your mouth in front of the lady."

Toledo backhanded Flint. The wrangler went flying. "Keep outta my business."

With a howl of fury, Flint launched himself at the other man. Toledo swung a punch that Andi was sure would knock Flint's head off, but the wrangler ducked and came up with both fists flailing.

A thick arm stopped Flint faster than a brick wall. "*¡Basta ya!*—that's enough," Cook growled, stepping between the two men. With his weight on his good leg, he gave Flint a shove that sent him sprawling toward the corral. "Tend to your stock, *chico.*" Then he turned to Toledo. "You will apologize to the *señorita.*"

Neither man looked eager to take on the formidable trail cook. Flint snatched his hat from the ground and scrambled away toward the corral. Toledo set his jaw, tipped his hat, and faced Andi. "Forgive me, Miss Carter." His apology sounded sincere, but his eyes held a mocking glint.

Andi nodded numbly. From the corner of her eye she saw Levi creeping away to follow Flint. She knew how he felt. She wanted to find a hole to crawl into. Mitch's words tickled her memory: *"Toledo's a loose cannon."*

Right now, that description fit the cocky cowhand like a glove.

I'm sorry I ever wanted to ride his horse . . . or to get to know him better, Andi thought. Sudden appreciation for grouchy old Cook welled up inside her. No wonder Mitch and Chad had few qualms about bringing their little sister along on a cattle drive—not if she stayed with Cook. His staunch defense of all things "proper" went a long way toward soothing Andi's trembling spirit.

The old man was not finished with Toledo. "Go wash up," he ordered, scowling darkly. "And stay away from the wrangler." His voice dropped. "And if I *ever* hear such coarse talk from you again in the presence of the *señorita*, I will beat you to a pulp. *¿Comprende?*"

The air crackled with tension. Toledo acknowledged Cook's warning with a stiff nod and snatched Sultan's reins out of Andi's hands.

Andi flinched, and her stomach turned over. "I'm sorry I took him without asking," she said in a tiny voice. "But you said I could ride him."

What was wrong with the young man? If he was worried about his precious horse's dirty legs, she'd be happy to take Sultan down to the river for a wash.

Toledo shot a wary glance toward Cook's retreating back then bent close to Andi's ear. "That's true, Miss Carter, but I require payment for his use." He winked and blew her a kiss. Before Andi could react to his impudence, Toledo yanked on Sultan's reins and led the horse off toward the river.

The outfit slowly recovered from the disastrous river crossing. By late afternoon weary, bruised, and bloodied cowhands began to stumble into camp. Cook immediately plied them with heaping plates of hot food and gallons of coffee—his universal cure-all for any ailment, physical or emotional. He also made his rounds of the injured, dabbing iodine on cuts and scrapes, checking for broken bones, and binding up Wyatt's sprained wrist.

In an extraordinary gesture of sympathy, Cook worked for more than an hour frying up a triple batch of hot, greasy doughnuts. Glassy eyes brightened at the sight of the pastries, and even the most worn-out man perked up and ate two or three. Levi downed four.

Andi nibbled on her first doughnut, too sick at heart to enjoy it. A couple of men, including Chad, were still out looking for stragglers; a few drovers circled the restless herd. The remainder of the somber group sat around the campfire evaluating their losses.

Out of a thousand cattle, nearly a hundred were missing or dead. Along the riverbank, a dozen steers, along with the odd horse here and there, lay trampled in the mud, their carcasses already beginning to swell under the blazing sun.

Worst of all, Bryce was dead. The young cowhand's battered body had washed ashore several hundred yards downriver, the victim of cattle gone crazy with fear. Another cowhand, Huey, was missing, but so far no trace of him or his horse had been found.

Tears leaked from Andi's eyes and trickled down her cheeks. Bryce had told the best campfire stories. He always kept everyone in stitches with his outrageous tales worthy of a dime novel. *Now he's dead, drowned in that rotten river.*

Andi couldn't pull her gaze away from the canvas-wrapped body lying underneath the chuck wagon. It waited for transport into Bakersfield then home to Bryce's family. A sob caught in her throat. *That could have been me or Levi.*

A shadow fell over her, and Andi looked up.

"May I join you?" Mitch asked. At Andi's nod, he sat down, wrapped a gentle arm around her shoulder, and squeezed. "I know this is hard," he said quietly, "but when it comes to a cattle drive, it's not usually a matter of *if*, but *when* for some kind of tragedy. Bryce knew the risks."

Andi let her tears come, hot and stinging. She barely knew Bryce. He wasn't a Circle C hand but one of the temporary drovers Mitch had recently hired.

It made no difference. She wept for him anyway. "Bryce had a m-mother and a father . . . and two little sisters," she sobbed. Her shoulders shook. "When I see him all wrapped up like that I think . . . I think . . ." She took a deep, shaky breath. "It could have been you or Chad or Levi . . . or even *me*."

Images of her and Levi's near-tragedy today swirled around in her head like the river water. She couldn't make the memory go away.

"But it *wasn't* any of us," Mitch said. He drew Andi closer. "Don't take it so hard, sis. You and Levi had your own close call. Then you wore yourself out helping to bring back the *remuda*. Like the rest of us, you've been dealt a pretty stiff blow. A decent night's sleep will help sort things out."

Andi bit her lip. He made it sound so easy.

Mitch brushed aside her escaped tangles and whispered in her ear, "I'm mighty proud of you for saving Levi's life today, but try to pull yourself together. Your grief is affecting the men." He held out a square of red cloth.

Andi glanced around. Mitch was right. The men looked embarrassed, at a loss on how to deal with the young, crying girl sitting across the campfire from them.

She choked back a fresh wave of sorrow. "I'll t-try." To prove it, she accepted Mitch's bandana and rubbed the tears from her hot, swollen face. "It's just too much to take in," she told him. "Bryce is dead, Huey's nowhere in sight; there's dead and missing cattle and those nine dead horses. Oh, Mitch, what will we do?"

Mitch chuckled. "That's the trail boss's worry, not yours, Miss Carter. We'll do fine, I expect. Chad and the others will show up with four or five dozen left-behinds. We'll get a good night's sleep and push south at dawn tomorrow."

He stood. "Life goes on, Andi. You know that. Now, eat your dough-nut like a good girl and give Cook a hand washing up." He winked at her. "Good job, by the way, getting those horses back."

Andi could only muster a watery smile for Mitch, but his praise did help dispel her gloom. A few minutes later, she was up to her elbows in suds, scrubbing tin plates and cups. She glanced up when two drov-ers arrived in camp and helped themselves to the half-empty plate of doughnuts. They looked done in.

"What's the news?" Mitch asked sharply.

"Found only a few head, boss," Kirby said. "We put 'em with the oth-ers." He sank to the ground and bit into a doughnut with obvious relish.

Mitch looked around then frowned. "Where's Chad?"

"What do you mean?" Kirby's eyebrows shot up. "He ain't here?"

Mitch shook his head.

"We split up," Seth put in. "He sent me and Kirby after the strag-glers so he could do some quick scouting farther south." He let out a disgusted breath. "Took us forever to find those dadblasted, ornery critters."

"Boss," Kirby said quietly, "Chad shoulda made it back here long before *we* did."

An eerie silence settled over the group. Andi stopped scrubbing; Levi put down the water buckets he was carrying.

Wyatt let out a long, low whistle. "Well, I reckon we'd best look for him before we lose the daylight."

Andi agreed. *But hurry!* she begged silently. The sun hung low on the western horizon.

CHAPTER 16

I've no time to write more than a quick prayer: Please, God! Help us find my brother!

"We'll split up and fan out south and west," Mitch ordered, buckling a six-shooter around his hips. From the back of the chuck wagon, Cook passed out revolvers to every drover not guarding the restless cattle.

"Where's mine?" Wyatt demanded.

"You've got a sprained wrist," Mitch said. "You need to take it easy until we get back."

"Listen here, boss," Wyatt insisted. "I'm a better cowpuncher with one arm than any of these yahoos are with two." He helped himself to a pistol and tucked it in his waistband. Then he chuckled. "Betcha my life Chad got waylaid in Bakersfield and is having himself a time."

"In that case, I will shoot him myself for worrying us," Diego grumbled.

The men laughed, but it sounded forced.

Andi stood next to the chuck wagon, her throat so tight it choked her. She knew no one really believed Chad had gone into Bakersfield. *So, where can he be? Why is Mitch handing out weapons?* A careless shot fired too close to the herd would stampede those dumb steers all over again.

Andi counted the scruffy, beat-up group of cowhands and her heart sank. Joselito, Tripp, and Toledo were out guarding the herd, so that left only Mitch, Diego, Wyatt, Seth, and Kirby to look for Chad. Unless they included Flint and Cook . . . *or me and Levi.*

Andi caught her breath. It would take a mighty big serving of sweet-talking, but it was worth a try. "You need all the help you can get, Mitch," she said, swallowing the lump that had settled in her throat. "I want to go along. Please?"

"No." He motioned to Flint and passed him a gun.

"Chad's my brother too!" Andi burst out. *No more sweet-talking.* "I can ride better than half this outfit." She didn't care that she'd just insulted the other drovers. "I won't get lost, not with the river so close." She paused. "And besides, who can miss all these cattle? You can see them for miles."

Mitch shook his head. "I'm sorry, Andi. You're exhausted and—"

"She's no more wore out than the rest of us," Flint cut in. "She's a good rider—better than me—and she's got sharp eyes. She found most of the scattered *remuda*. You'd be a fool not to take her along, boss."

Murmurs of agreement rippled among the men.

"Another set of eyes would be mighty useful," Kirby added. He thumbed toward Wyatt. "You're lettin' this one-armed, useless cowpuncher go along."

Andi listened in astonishment. For once, she was being treated like a valuable member of this outfit and not as *Miss Carter*, the boss's sister. She set aside the emotional fatigue that threatened to overwhelm her and straightened her shoulders. *Listen to them, Mitch*, she pleaded silently. *Because if you don't, I'm going anyway.*

Andi would find herself in a heap of trouble if she defied the trail boss and set out to find Chad on her own. Mitch would stuff her on the first train out of Bakersfield. Her heart thudded at the gruesome vision, but being sent home in disgrace was worth the price of finding Chad. He might ride into camp an hour from now, feeling fresh as a spring morning, but Andi would not regret her decision to help out—with or without Mitch's say-so.

Mitch looked as surprised as Andi felt. He stared at his drovers, pondering. Then he turned his gaze on Andi. She stared back at him, unflinching.

"Looks like I've been outvoted," Mitch said at last. He gave Andi a crooked smile.

She relaxed and breathed a quiet, *Thank you, Lord!*

"I don't have time to stand around and argue." Mitch placed a heavy revolver in Andi's sweaty palm. "If you come across Chad and he's hurt, fire three shots." He looked out at the others. "That goes for the rest of you too. The sun's going down. Let's find out what happened to our ramrod."

"What about me, Uncle Mitch?" Levi piped up. "I ain't much of a cowhand, but you know I can ride real good. And my eyes are as sharp as Andi's." He straightened to his full height. "I'm as tall as Andi too. What's more, I'm a bo—"

"Kate will have my hide if I give you a pistol," Mitch said. "But you can grab a horse and join the search."

"I shoot fine," Levi objected. "You taught me yourself." He changed his tune at Mitch's frown. "I don't need one, I guess." He scuffed the dust with his boot toe then hightailed it to the *remuda* for a horse before his uncle changed his mind.

—·—

When Mitch said "fan out," he meant it. Andi could no longer see anyone from their outfit. She could barely make out the dark smudge of the herd she'd left far behind to the north. With the sun on her right and just touching the tops of thick oak groves to the west, she nudged Dusty and scanned the open spaces ahead of her for any movement.

With her whole heart Andi wanted to be the one to find her brother. Not just because it would prove she could carry her own weight, but because she wanted to be the first to see that Chad was all right. "Of course he's all right," she told herself. He was too ornery to let anybody or anything get the best of him.

"His horse probably went lame or threw a shoe," she told Dusty. Then she cringed. "Here I am confiding in *you*—a scruffy, no-account cow pony—just like I would Taffy." She sighed. Talking to an equine companion always helped her think things through. Taffy would understand.

"Chad's probably furious at having to walk all the way back to camp with a limping, useless pony trailing behind him."

It was not a pretty picture. A cowpuncher's boots were high-heeled, pointed, and geared toward keeping his feet in the stirrups, not for walking long distances. "Fuming mad and hurting bad," Andi muttered. "Maybe I *don't* want to run into him first."

Her gut tensed. The alternative was unthinkable. "You can holler at me as much as you like," she yelled. "Just so long as you're in one piece to do it." She listened. Evening birds chirped from scattered valley oaks, and swallows swooped overhead. "Chad! Where are you?"

Dusty tugged impatiently at the reins, and Andi turned west, splashing through one of the dozens of shallow creeks that trickled through this part of the valley. The streams flowed south and eventually drained into Buena Vista Lake, according to Chad. "Did he scout clear to the lake?" she asked Dusty. She didn't dare venture that far, not with the sun going down so quickly.

Worry for Chad spurred Andi onward. She weaved her way across a three-mile strip, trotting through clearings and slowing down when she came across a stand of trees and thick vegetation. She poked her head through the thickets of willow and oak but didn't stay long. Twilight settled over the forest, casting a gloomy light through the heavy canopy. She shivered and kneed Dusty to hurry him along.

Walk, trot, walk. Andi fell into the rhythm of the cow pony's steady gait, and her mind wandered. As much as she enjoyed riding instead of sitting on the chuck wagon's hard seat, she wished she were home. *There, I said it*, Andi thought. *I want to go home.*

Was it only this morning when she'd finally gotten off her mental seesaw and decided to stick out the rest of the drive? Impossible! It felt like days had passed since she'd told herself a Carter never quits.

Andi yawned and rubbed her gritty, stinging eyes. "I am going to have to reconsider that statement," she told Dusty.

Feeling dizzy at her emotional ups and downs, her thoughts seesawed again. *Who cares if Levi "wins" and I go home?* Pesky tears pooled, but she blinked them back. The river crossing and Bryce's drowning had hit her hard, pushing the cattle-drive notion clean out of her head forever.

All she had to do now was humble herself and admit she wasn't cut out for this work. "I think I'll stick to being a rancher's sister, or even a rancher's wife. There's no shame in staying home and raising . . . horses. No sirree. Driving ornery cattle to market is nothing but hard, dirty work—" She caught her breath. Hadn't Mother said those very words to her less than two weeks ago?

"As soon as we find Chad and make sure he's all right, I'm going to take Mitch up on his offer to put me on the train in Bakersfield." Saying the words aloud cemented them in Andi's tired mind. She reined Dusty to the south and started another sweep of the nearby countryside. The light was quickly fading. Yawning again, she slumped and rode on.

Oof! Andi's eyes flew open when she hit the ground hard. Inches away from her face, a big, black beetle skittered through the grass. She flung herself upright and looked around. Dusty, that disloyal beast, was twenty yards away, keeping up his plodding pace as if his rider was still mounted.

I didn't even feel that fall! Andi staggered to her feet and ran after her horse. "You could've at least stopped," she scolded him when she caught up.

Dusty pinned back his ears and whinnied. It sounded like a laugh. Andi snagged the dangling reins and tugged the pony to a standstill so she could mount. "It's not funny." She smacked him on the neck and climbed into the saddle.

Dusty snorted, sidestepped, and shook his dirty, tangled mane.

A sudden explosion of gunfire shattered the quiet evening. Dusty reared and came down at a full run. Two more shots followed the first.

"Somebody found Chad!" Andi squealed. She hung on and sawed at Dusty's mouth to turn him. "The shots came from *this* way," she insisted when he fought the bit. "Run as fast as you want, but run *east*." One more fierce tug on the reins and Dusty gave in. He turned and galloped where Andi directed.

In the distance, Andi saw three faraway riders converging on a copse of oaks. Two more appeared from the north. *But I'm the closest!* She had never whipped a horse in her life, but she did so now. She slapped the ends of her reins across Dusty's backside and yelled, *"Move!"*

Dusty flattened his ears and lengthened his stride. As they drew up to the trees, Andi noticed large, black, winged objects circling overhead. The hair on the back of her neck stood up.

Buzzards! Oh, no!

CHAPTER 17

I thought I was tired before we crossed the river today. After nearly drowning, fetching back the horses, and searching for Chad, I could barely keep my eyes open. All I wanted to do was sleep. But now I'm so frightened I know I won't close my eyes all night.

Thanks to Dusty's headlong plunge, Andi arrived well ahead of the other riders. She hauled her lathered horse to a stop so quickly that he sat down. Andi threw the reins aside and fell from the saddle, landing on the ground with a painful *thud*. The sudden, sharp jab in her gut reminded her that her waistband still held the pistol Mitch had given her. She winced and pulled it free. Then she rushed over to where Diego squatted next to a crumpled body.

Andi stopped short, setting the gun out of her way. "Is he . . . is he . . ." Fingers of fear curled around her thoughts and kept her from saying the dreaded word aloud.

Diego glanced up. His dark eyes looked haunted. One hand was pressed against Chad's side. "No, *señorita*, he is not dead. But he is badly hurt. He needs a doctor *pronto*."

Andi's relief was short-lived. "Badly hurt? How? What happened? Did he fall off his horse?" She looked around. Not far away, a sorrel gelding stood quietly, as though waiting for his rider to remount.

Andi sank to the ground beside Diego and stifled a cry. Chad would not be remounting anytime soon. He lay unconscious in a pool of blood. A deep gash sliced across the side of his head. She reached out to shake him, but Diego gripped her arm.

"Do not touch him, *señorita*," he said. "Not until Cook arrives to look him over."

Andi nodded and let her trembling hand fall limply to her side. "Did his horse throw him?" The cut on his head looked as if he'd knocked himself out on a rock when he fell.

"I do not think so," Diego said grimly. "This was not an accident. I think *Señor* Chad was bushwhacked, and not long ago. Take a look." He motioned toward Chad's upper body.

For the first time, Andi focused on what Diego was doing. A ragged hole had ripped through Chad's vest and shirt. The Mexican drover held a wadded piece of blood-soaked fabric against a wound in Chad's side.

"It's a gunshot!" Andi fell backward. Visions of Mitch being shot almost two years ago slammed into her mind. "No, no, *no!*"

I can't do this again! Andi shook all over. *I can't watch another brother hang between life and death.* The world spun. Black dots filled her vision. Right then she knew she was going to swoon . . . just like a prissy girl. She couldn't prevent it. Mental anguish and exhaustion from the past few days merged to shut her down once and for all. She closed her eyes.

Diego's fingers clamped down painfully on Andi's shoulder. She yelped, fully awake. "Not now. You must stay with your brother and keep pressure on the wound." He drew Andi closer and showed her how to press the cloth against Chad's side and keep it there. "Do not let up. I will ride like the wind to fetch Cook." He motioned at the quickly approaching riders. "You will not be alone for long."

Dazed, Andi nodded.

"Bueno." Diego sprang to his feet, raced to his horse, and swung into the saddle. He bent low over the cow pony's neck and took off north, toward camp.

Andi watched him go until the twilight swallowed him up. Then she shook herself free of the mind-numbing cobwebs and took three deep breaths to keep from blacking out. Swallowing hard, she forced herself to look at the hand holding the bloody cloth. Her fingers were already red. She turned away and squeezed her eyes shut.

Dear God, she prayed. *This can't be happening. But it is. I can't faint. Or cry. Keep me strong. No hysterics. Thank You that Chad's alive and that I don't have to do the doctoring this time. Thank You that Diego found him first. I probably would have fired the three shots and waited around while Chad slowly bled to death.*

A wave of relief that Mitch would soon be here to take over—along with Cook and the others—chased the helplessness from Andi's mind. She heard the thundering of approaching hooves and looked up to see Mitch rein his horse and vault out of the saddle. His face was chalk white.

"What happened?" he demanded in a harsh tone.

Shivers ran up and down Andi's spine. She had never heard Mitch speak like that before. She wished Diego was here to give Mitch the devastating news, but it was up to her. "Chad's been shot."

Mitch sucked in his breath and dropped down beside Andi. The rest of the riders closed in but gave him plenty of room. He quickly pulled out his handkerchief and wadded it up. "Let me," he said.

Andi didn't need to be told twice. She gratefully withdrew her stained hand and scooted out of the way. Mitch pressed the new cloth on top of the old one and held it down. "Looks like a flesh wound," he said. "Serious, but not life-threatening." He smiled at Andi, but his smile didn't reach his eyes.

"Don't you *dare* lie to me, Mitch Carter," Andi scolded. "You're scared. I can tell."

Chad moaned, rescuing Mitch from having to answer. Instead, he nodded toward the disappearing rider. "Was that Diego who rode off for Cook?"

Andi nodded.

Mitch shaded his eyes and looked west. "Sun's nearly gone. I don't want to move Chad, so I reckon we'll move the camp to him." He frowned then fired off instructions like a Gatling gun. "Flint, bring the *remuda* here and corral them before it gets too dark."

"Sure thing, boss."

Mitch pointed to Levi, who had not yet dismounted. Eyes wide and unblinking, the boy looked glued to his saddle. "Go with Flint, Levi. Do whatever he tells you."

Levi jerked from his trancelike state and nodded. The two galloped away.

"I hate to move those beeves," Mitch said, looking around at his men. "They're spooked enough. But I want them brought as close as possible to our new camp before we lose the light." He looked at Wyatt. "You're in charge."

"Right, boss," Wyatt said. "We'll push 'em best we can then bed 'em down. Won't hurt us none to change shifts and sleep out with the herd this one night."

Mitch nodded his approval. "Get to it."

The small group pointed their horses toward camp and left in a pounding wave, churning up grass and dirt.

Andi watched the men and horses fade into the deepening twilight. Then she turned back to Mitch. "What about me? What do you want me to do?"

"I want you to stay with me," Mitch said. "When my hand gets tired of holding this rag, I'll trade places with you."

Andi hoped Cook would arrive before that happened. She rubbed her hands alongside her britches. The blood didn't come off. She shuddered.

Night closed in. Andi settled herself on the ground next to Chad and curled into a tight ball. She watched her brother's chest rise and fall while a thousand frogs sang a background chorus. *Please, Lord, keep Your hand on Chad. Don't let him bleed to death.*

What seemed like half the night later—but must really have been less than an hour—Andi woke to the rattling and banging of the approaching chuck wagon. She sat up, straining to see through the velvet darkness.

The sky was a dark, navy blue. The sun had definitely set, but the waning moon would not rise until after midnight.

A small glow of yellow lantern-light grew closer, accompanied by loud clattering and the sound of Cook urging the horses even faster. He yahooed, and Mitch called back, "Over here!"

"How did he know how to find us?" Andi asked in awe.

"Diego must have told him right where we were, and Cook's sense of direction is uncanny." Mitch chuckled at Andi's skeptical look. "Besides, I lit a fire." He indicated the small, crackling blaze several yards away. "Did you get some rest?"

Andi shook her head. She felt groggier than ever. She looked at Chad, who had not yet awakened. Fear licked at her. "Tell me the truth, Mitch," she whispered. "Is he going to be all right? He's not going to die like . . . like . . . Bryce, is he?"

"I promise you he'll be fine, so long as no infection sets in," Mitch said. "He's breathing easier, and his wound doesn't look too bad."

Andi didn't know how Mitch could say that. Chad's gunshot injury looked pretty bad to her, mixed in with all that blood. She sent up a quick prayer that it would stay clean. *No infection . . . please!*

Cook pulled the chuck wagon to a stop and put the two men with him to work. In no time, a pot of water hung over the fire to boil and Cook found his bundle of medical supplies. He motioned Mitch aside and hovered over Chad, mumbling irately in Spanish at whomever had done such a thing to *Señor* Chad. The only words he said in English were directed at the men. "Unload the wagon so it can hold the *señor*."

Toledo and Seth emptied the chuck wagon, set up camp, then sat around the fire. Toledo took over the job of making coffee and shortly had everyone's cup filled to the brim. After satisfying their bellies with the hot brew, the two cowhands crept back to their night-guard posts with the cattle.

One by one, other drovers drifted into the new camp for coffee and news of Chad. The herd had been settled no more than a quarter mile away. The horses were safely corralled nearby. Mitch looked visibly relieved.

The Mexican cowhands, Joselito and Diego, paused over Chad and mumbled a quick prayer before going on. *"Gracias,"* Mitch said softly. Two other Circle C hands followed suit then melted into the night. Soon, only Cook and the Carters were left at the new camp.

Andi looked around for Levi and found him in his usual place under the wagon, fast asleep. A sudden urge to curl up beside him and forget the here and now washed over her, but she knew she wouldn't be able to sleep. Adrenaline still surged through her veins. She stayed near Cook and held her breath, anxious to hear the prognosis.

"I removed the bullet and bandaged both wounds," Cook finally said. *"Señor* Chad has lost a lot of blood, but the bullet missed his stomach and only bit into his flesh. It looks messy, but it is not as bad as I feared. I would say he was shot from his horse and then hit his head on a rock." Cook sat back on his heels and smiled. "When he wakes up, *ay!* He will have the mother of all headaches."

As if on cue, Chad groaned and came to. "Where—what?" He tried to sit up, but his face twisted with pain and he fell back to the ground.

"That oughta teach you," Mitch scolded. "Lie still and be grateful you're alive."

"Gracias a Dios," Cook said, crossing himself. "There is little doubt the Mighty One had you in His sights today."

Chad let out a long, slow breath. His fingers explored his bandaged head. He winced. "I don't know what hurts worse"—he paused for breath—"my head or my belly." He looked around with glazed eyes.

Cook disappeared and returned with a small, dark bottle and a spoon. "Laudanum will help the pain."

Chad batted the medicine away. "Not yet." Sweat broke out on his face, showing Andi that her brother hurt a whole lot more than he let on. "Go after them," he said, closing his eyes. He sucked in a painful breath. "They shot me and . . . stole our beef . . ." His voice trailed off.

"Who?" Mitch demanded.

Chad didn't answer. He slipped into unconsciousness with a tired sigh.

CHAPTER 18

I think it's my fault that Chad was shot. Levi and I saw two strangers camped out the other day, and I never told Mitch. Toledo said they were just passing through, and I believed him. I reckon they fooled Toledo too.

Between sips of Cook's "special" brew—laced with laudanum, Andi suspected—Chad roused long enough to tell them what he knew. Bit by bit, his tragic story unfolded.

"They got lucky," Chad whispered. "The river crossing played right into their hands. The scattered herd . . . losing Bryce . . ." He grimaced but insisted he felt well enough to sit up and lean against the wagon wheel.

When Cook refused, Chad tried to do it himself. He boosted himself on his elbows and started scooting toward the wagon. He made it two feet before collapsing to the ground.

"Of all the hardheaded stunts . . ." Mitch's voice trailed off. He shook his head in disgust. "Are you *trying* to bleed to death, big brother? Why can't you just stay put, at least until daybreak?"

"Help . . . me . . . up," Chad said between clenched teeth.

Mitch and Cook exchanged resigned looks then carefully guided Chad to an upright position against the wheel. By the time he was settled, Chad was panting, and drops of sweat glistened on his forehead.

Andi bit down hard on her lip to keep from crying out. When would that laudanum take effect?

Chad closed his eyes, winced, then gathered his strength to go on. "I scouted south after I sent Kirby and Seth to round up the stragglers. I don't think the thieves expected me to run into them." Through cracked lips, he managed a smile. "I surprised them. Winged one of 'em before they plugged me."

"How many?" Mitch asked.

Chad took a deep breath, and his face contorted in agony. "Three men; at least seventy-five steers, maybe more. They were driving them east like they owned 'em." He coughed suddenly. The movement made him cry out and plunge forward.

Mitch caught Chad before he fell and gently guided him back to the wagon wheel. "Take it easy. You've told us enough."

Chad coughed and clutched his bandaged middle until Cook forced a cup of water into him. Chad took two gulps and pushed the cup away. "No, I haven't." When the hacking fit passed, his pain-filled gaze bored into Mitch. "Two were strangers, one fella with a handlebar mustache and the other with a mop of black hair." His face hardened. "The third one was . . . Huey."

Andi's heart hammered against the inside of her chest. "Huey? One of *our* drovers?"

Chad nodded. Before he could add anything more, the laudanum took effect. He blinked and tried to stay awake, but his head lolled onto his chest. Cook and Mitch lowered Chad to the ground and covered him up.

Cook flicked a satisfied smile at Mitch. "That took longer than I thought it would, but the medicine should keep him quiet for a few hours."

"I hope so," Mitch said. "I have to make plans. Chad needs better care than we can give him here."

"*Sí,*" Cook heartily agreed.

"And I've got all that beef to move." Mitch sighed. "We can't stick around here for days, waiting for Chad to heal."

"There is also the chance he might insist he is fine and try to drag himself into his saddle tomorrow morning," Cook said ominously.

Mitch furrowed his brow. "He just might."

Cook laid a rough, wrinkled hand on Mitch's shoulder and said, "Do not concern yourself, *Señor* Mitch. I will take him to Bakersfield tonight. It is not far." He rose and gave Mitch an amused look. "But your brother will be *muy enojado* when he awakens and finds himself bedridden and trussed up like a new calf." He chuckled.

"He'll just have to be mad," Mitch said, frowning. "You can tell Chad he's no good to me in his condition. He might as well rest while he can. We'll pick him up on the way home." Mitch scratched his chin and counted to himself. Andi saw his lips moving. "A week and a half, maybe two. Should be about right."

"*Sí, señor,*" Cook said. "I will return as soon as I can."

While Mitch and Cook settled Chad's fate for the next several days, Andi sat quietly on the ground, pondering. Her thoughts reeled at the knowledge Huey had betrayed them and helped steal their cattle. But Huey's involvement didn't drain the blood from Andi's face like Chad's description of the other two thieves.

Black hair? Handlebar mustache? Andi was tempted to shake Levi awake so he could refresh her memory. Not even a week ago they'd spied on two drifters who matched that description. Why hadn't she told Mitch?

The answer prompted Andi to kick herself mentally. Because she'd let the handsome Toledo soothe her worries with his fancy stunt riding and smooth talking. *Is he in on it too?*

Andi shook her head to rid herself of such thoughts. "If Toledo was in on it, would he still be *here?*" she asked herself. "Of course not. He would have vanished. It's not his fault. It's *mine.*" She moaned. "I should never have come on this cattle drive."

"Andi, who are you talking to?" Mitch yanked her from her dismal thoughts. He stood over her, his arms folded across his chest, regarding her with concern. Behind him, Cook reached over the side of his half-empty chuck wagon. He tucked a blanket around Chad's still form. Next to him in the wagon bed lay the canvas-draped form of Bryce's body.

"Oh, Mitch!" Andi cried, leaping to her feet. "This is all my fault. I saw those men last week—the ones Chad described—when you sent me to wash up in the pond. I should have told you, but—"

"Hold it right there," Mitch ordered. He raised a hand to interrupt her chatter. "I told Cook that Chad's no use to me all shot up. Now, I'm telling *you* that you're no use to me if you go into hysterics over something that can't be changed. I know you're exhausted and overwrought, worn out from a week of hard work, little sleep, and unexpected disaster—not to mention falling victim to a mosquito attack. So I understand the fool's talk. But it has to stop."

Andi felt her pulse quicken. She had heard nothing past *"you're no use to me."* What was Mitch saying? Would he send her to Bakersfield with Chad? If he couldn't use her on the drive any longer, then it only made sense to send her home. She took a deep breath. *And isn't that what I want?*

Yes. It was exactly what she wanted. This was her chance to leave. She'd made the decision this evening while riding Dusty around, hopelessly searching for her missing brother. *I was going to ask Mitch to send me home, anyway*, she reminded herself. Now, she could stay in Bakersfield and care for Chad until the drive was over. It would be a relief.

"Andi!"

Andi jumped, startled. "W-what?"

"Have you heard anything I said?"

No, she hadn't. Her thoughts had been in Bakersfield, not out here in the middle of the valley. "Uh . . . you're sending me into town with Chad?"

In the red flow of the firelight, Mitch's look turned incredulous. "Where in the world did you get an idea like *that*?"

Cook's loud guffaw confirmed that Andi had missed everything Mitch said. The old man climbed into the driver's seat, hung a second lantern on a hook, and jiggled the reins. *"Hasta mañana, señor.* I hope to return before sunrise to prepare breakfast."

"Wait!" Andi called out in confusion. Her ride was getting ready to melt into the night. She would be left behind.

Cook pulled back on the reins and gave Andi a puzzled look.

She turned to Mitch. "You're . . ." She swallowed. "You're not sending me home?"

Mitch let out a deep breath and rubbed his forehead, clearly trying to stay awake. "On the contrary, Andi, I'm promoting you to wrangler." He motioned beyond the chuck wagon, where Andi could hear snuffling and quiet snorting. "I want you to check on the *remuda* and then get to bed. We have a long week ahead of us." He pawed through a pile of extra supplies and tossed her a dark object. "You'll need a new hat."

Andi caught the headgear. "Me? Wrangler? What about Flint?"

"He'll be punching cows for the rest of the drive," Mitch said. "Right now he's taking his turn at night guard."

Andi's mind spun out of control. She felt like she'd just been tossed back in the Kern River, swimming for her life, trying to draw breath. Her throat tightened. *I just want to go home!* "But w-why?" she stammered.

Mitch didn't answer. He nodded to Cook, and the wagon rolled away.

Andi watched it go, completely drained. Mitch was turning this cattle drive upside down. "What will Mother say when she finds out I'm no longer Cook's—"

"Mother's not here," Mitch said in a weary voice. He seemed more drained than Andi. "In case you haven't noticed, we are severely short-handed."

Sudden realization slammed into Andi like a railroad engine, knocking the words out of her. Chad was injured and out of the picture; Bryce was dead; Huey had deserted; Wyatt had a sprained wrist. She looked up at Mitch in dismay. "What will you do?" she whispered.

"Just what I'm doing now. Rearranging things. I've always known you could handle the horses as well as—or better than—Flint. Mother will understand when she learns why." He gestured to where Levi lay sleeping. The wagon had rolled right above him without waking him. "Levi has to grow up some tomorrow too. He's going to join Flint riding drag."

Andi stood speechless. *This is a bad dream. I'm too tired to do this for another week or more.* Her ears caught the fading sounds of the chuck wagon, and she sighed.

"What's troubling you?" Mitch frowned his concern.

I can't let him know how miserable I am, Andi thought. He would send her with Chad, after all, and end up with even less help.

"Afraid you can't do the job?" Mitch asked. "I'm not worried. After all, you're a Carter." He squeezed her shoulder. "Let's not have any more crazy talk about how or why Chad came to be injured. Do you hear me?"

Mitch's words chased Andi's guilt into a small, unused corner of her mind. She could think about it later, after the drive was over. "I hear you," she said.

Andi pitied Levi. He'd soon be tossed headfirst into prodding the slow-pokes of the herd. He was only a boy. Then she caught herself. *What are you talking about, Andi Carter? You just got tossed headfirst into being a wrangler!* It was exactly the job she'd begged for when she'd sat around the supper table the week before the drive, filled to the brim with energy and so cocksure of herself.

I know better now. Andi swallowed her piece of humble pie. She no longer wanted the wrangler job, but here was her chance to pitch in and make a success of the drive. Greenhorn or not, tired or not, miserable or not, Andi would wrangle those horses the best she could. She'd do it because her brother was counting on her, and she wouldn't let him down.

For the last time, Andi climbed off her disturbing, mental seesaw . . . and threw it away.

A Carter never quits.

CHAPTER 19

I have done the figuring and come up short. I don't know how a girl, a half-grown boy, a green wrangler-turned-cowpuncher, and a one-armed drover can possibly take the place of grown, able-bodied men. Worse, I think the cattle know we're shorthanded.

For the first time since the cattle drive began, Andi woke to the sun shining in her face. With a gasp, she flung her covers aside and sat up. *What's wrong? Why are we still here?* She dug her grimy fists into her eyes and rubbed the sleep away.

Gathering up her bedroll, Andi crammed it into a wrinkled ball and stashed it on the ground next to her saddle. Then she looked around. Where was Mitch? Where was Levi? Where was *anybody*?

Not far away to the south, a dark mass of cattle grazed contentedly. Andi could make out ten figures on horseback circling the herd, keeping the steers together. She counted the riders and realized Levi was out there too, getting a crash course in prodding cattle.

She glanced east. It was at least an hour past sunrise. Why wasn't the outfit on the move? Levi and Flint could easily practice their new roles while the cattle were plodding along. Then she remembered that Mitch was waiting for Cook's return. She turned back to the camp.

Last night's embers burned hot and bright this morning; signs of an improvised breakfast lay everywhere. Someone had scrounged the left-behind supplies and attempted to stir up something to eat. A black pot hung from a tripod over the fire.

Andi hurried to the pot, peeked in, and made a face. Beans. She found a clean plate and dished herself up a small serving—just enough to keep her hunger pangs in check. The beans crunched between her teeth, and somebody had forgotten the salt. She choked them down.

"I miss Cook," she muttered between bites. "How long can it take to go to town and back?" She shaded her eyes and squinted in the direction of Bakersfield, many miles to the northeast. In the distance, Andi spied the familiar sight of a wagon and two horses. The white canvas cover flapped in the breeze. As usual, Cook was not sparing the horses.

Horses! Andi caught her breath. "I'm the wrangler!"

She pitched her plate and fork into the washtub with the rest of the dirty, piled-up dishes. Then she snagged her hat and spurred into action. Her saddle lay where she'd used it as a pillow. She lugged it to the temporary corral near a stand of oaks. Dropping the saddle to the ground, she looked the *remuda* over. There seemed to be twice as many horses in daylight than when she'd checked on them last night.

The enormity of this new responsibility made Andi gulp. Without well-fed and rested horses, the cattle drive would come to a standstill. *I'm really in charge of keeping all of these horses cared for.* She tightened her fingers around the rope corral. "Howdy, fellas."

At her voice, several cow ponies looked up before going back to cropping grass. Andi tried not to think about the handful of horses that had not survived the river crossing. She chewed on her lip, unsure of her wrangler duties. She couldn't ask Flint. He was long gone, well on his way to becoming a drag rider or—with a little luck or skill—eventually a swing or flank rider.

I better figure out double-quick how to handle this lot.

A shadow fell over Andi, and she jerked from her thoughts. Toledo stood a few feet away, watching her.

"Don't sneak up on me!" she hollered.

"Whoa, but you're jumpy this morning." He grinned. "But I reckon I'd be jumpy too if I had your job."

Andi gave him a puzzled look.

"Heard you're the new wrangler," Toledo said. "It's about time. You can't do worse than that tinhorn Flint. Thanks to his bumbling, you're stuck with the orneriest *remuda* on God's green earth." His smile widened. "But you can handle it."

Andi wasn't sure what to make of Toledo. When they'd crossed paths yesterday, he nearly bit her head off. Now he was back to his charming, strutting self. She scowled. "What do you want?"

"What do you *think* I want from the wrangler?" He chuckled. "A fresh horse. My turn at night duty was longer than either Sultan or I like."

"Help yourself," Andi told him. "You know which horse string is yours." *Because I sure don't*, she added silently.

Toledo talked nonstop as he pulled his saddle off Sultan and tossed it on a dark chestnut gelding. Most of his words blasted Flint's inexperience, with a few barbs sprinkled in about the general mishandling of the drive. The final blow fell when Toledo hinted that the current leadership could be blamed for yesterday's calamities, including Bryce's untimely death.

Andi's anger blazed. How dare he find fault with her brothers! "You talk mighty big, Mr. McGuire. I suppose you could do a better job as trail boss?"

"Most assuredly, *Miss Andi*," he drawled.

The way he said her name, and the way his gaze swept over her sent eerie chills racing up and down her arms. The fact that Mitch and Cook—and the rest of the men—were away from camp added to her uneasiness. She tugged her hat down on her forehead and bent over for her saddle. "I've got work to do."

Toledo slapped Sultan on the rump. The horse made a beeline for the *remuda*. Then the drover reached around Andi and hoisted her saddle with one hand. "Let me help you with that."

"I can do it myself."

"I insist," Toledo said.

Andi had no choice. She would lose a tug-of-war with the brawny cowhand. Seething, she let go and watched Toledo sling her saddle onto Dusty and cinch it up. He turned to give her a sweeping bow. "There you go, Miss Wrangler."

"Thank you," Andi forced out.

Toledo mounted the chestnut. "Mind you look after my horse. And no more riding off on him without my say-so, ya hear?"

Andi stiffened at the taunt.

Toledo gave her a mocking, two-fingered salute. "By the way, it looks like these ponies could use some water." He slapped his horse with his knotted rope-end and galloped back to the herd.

The childish urge to pick up a rock and pitch it at Toledo's stiff back engulfed Andi. "Why did I ever think he was so charming and good-looking?" Fingers fumbling in fury, she bridled Dusty. It would take some doing, but she determined to let Toledo's conceited remarks fly over her head without settling. If not, she might be tempted to wish he and Bryce could change places!

"All right, Dusty, you ugly plug," she said, clearing her mind from troubling thoughts. "Let's get to work."

Dusty never looked excited to let a rider mount him, and this morning was no exception. Andi scrambled into the saddle before he could kick or shy away. When he felt her weight on his back, he flattened his ears and crow-hopped a couple of times.

Andi quickly put a stop to that. "I wish you'd quit this nonsense. You know I'm your only friend. Nobody else—especially Flint—can stand to even look at you."

Dusty shook his head and tried a few zigzag tricks to dump his rider. When Andi didn't budge, he looked at her as if to say, "All right, you win this time," and settled down.

Andi had ridden the scruffy gelding more than once over the past several days, but she'd never asked him to herd cattle or horses. By the time she drove the *remuda* to the creek, she discovered that under his homely, mean exterior, Dusty was worth his weight in gold. When Andi nudged him toward a straying horse, he took over. One nip, and the drifter immediately fell into place. Her respect for the cow pony grew by leaps and bounds.

The horses drank their fill. A few minutes later, Andi and Dusty bunched them together in a new grazing spot. "It's too bad Flint didn't discover how well you can boss the *remuda*," Andi told him. "All he had to do was make friends and learn how to boss *you*."

Smiling, Andi turned Dusty in with the rest of the horses and dog-trotted back to camp. Her smile faded when she saw the chuck wagon. The horses had been unharnessed and were picketed nearby, grazing. She hurried over, dreading to hear bad news. "Is Chad all right?"

"*Sí, señorita*," Cook said. "He has strict orders from Dr. Frazier to stay in bed for the rest of the week." A smile split his dark, wrinkled face. "*Señora* Stewart, who runs the boardinghouse, will make sure your brother follows the doctor's instructions." He chuckled. "I have no doubts she can accomplish this."

When Andi didn't respond, Cook laid a gentle hand on her head. "*No se preocupe*. He is in no danger."

Andi's throat tightened in gratitude. Tears pricked her eyes. *Thank You, God*, she prayed. Then she threw her arms around Cook's neck and brushed a quick kiss across his leathery cheek. "*Muchas, muchas gracias,*" she whispered.

Cook coughed and cleared his throat. "*De nada*," he said gruffly, untangling Andi's arms. "Enough of this." But his eyes glistened at her show of affection. He swiped the back of his hand across his face when Mitch approached. "*Lo siento, señor,*" he apologized. "The marshes delayed my journey. I feared I would never find my way around those swamps."

Mitch waved away Cook's apology. "It couldn't be helped. So long as Chad is in good hands." When Cook nodded, Mitch launched into business. "All right then. We'll break camp as soon as you're packed up. We can probably make ten miles today if we push it."

Packed up. Andi's weary heart sank as she scanned the area. Supplies littered the ground. With a resigned sigh, she bent over and picked up the washtub stacked high with dirty plates and cups.

"*¡Ay, no!*" Cook scolded. He limped over to Andi and took the washtub away. "You are a wrangler now, *chica*, and will not do dishes. Neither will Levi."

"But . . ." Andi's voice trailed off. How would Cook manage by himself? He couldn't fix meals, do dishes, haul water, and find firewood all on his own. Not to mention his extra duties of sewing the constant rips and tears in the drovers' clothes and repairing broken equipment. *He needs Levi and me.*

Just then, a small, dark-haired boy darted into view from around the back of the wagon. His arms were piled high with wood. He dumped his load in front of Cook. "Is this enough, *Tío* Manuel?" he asked in lisping Spanish.

Cook grunted and sent the boy to fetch more. "My sister's grandson," he explained when Mitch raised his eyebrows. "Rico is a good boy, used to hard work. He will help me, freeing up the *señorita* and Levi for more important tasks."

Mitch brightened. "*Gracias.* I wasn't sure how I was going to shuffle duties between night guard, day jobs, and help for you."

"The problem is now solved," Cook replied.

No more was said about young Rico. He slid smoothly into place as Cook's right hand. From what Andi could see, the skinny Mexican boy worked harder than she and Levi combined. He was a whirlwind of nonstop motion but spoke little. His willingness to scramble around at Cook's bidding for sixteen hours a day put Andi to shame.

Knowing they had ten miles to cover, Andi prepared herself for a long day. Watering the *remuda* near camp was one thing. Keeping them together on the trail, giving them grazing time, and trading fresh horses for the drovers' spent mounts was something entirely different. She'd seen Flint run himself ragged trying to manage the horse herd.

"Partner," she said when she mounted Dusty an hour later. "Show me you can boss the horses as well as you did this morning, and I'll bring you a biscuit tonight." He snorted and tossed his mane but for once stood still.

By late afternoon, Dusty had earned a dozen biscuits. Andi's backside was sore from sitting in the saddle all day, but not as sore as bouncing on the chuck wagon's hard seat. She'd barely secured the *remuda* behind the rope corral when Mitch trotted up.

"You and that pony make a good team," he praised her, relaxing in his saddle.

"Thanks. Dusty does all the work."

"Are you two up to giving Levi and Flint a hand?" Mitch's mouth was set in a grim line. "They're having more than their fair share of trouble. Dusty could help move the drag along."

"Sure." Andi shrugged, trying not to betray her disappointment.

"Atta girl!" Mitch smiled. "It's a dirty job, and I'm sorry, but I can't spare anybody else." He turned and raced back to the herd.

Andi looked with weary longing at the campsite Cook and Rico were setting up. She'd managed the *remuda* well. More than anything she wanted to rest and enjoy the fruits of her labor. Instead, Mitch had rewarded her with more work.

If Mother could see me now . . .

Her thought trailed off as she pulled Dusty out for one more round. Up until today, the herd had trailed behind their leaders like elephants in a parade. A quick move from a trail hand or a crack from Toledo's knotted rope kept the slowpokes moving.

Not any longer. When the tail end of the herd came into sight, Andi sagged. It was as if the wily steers knew a couple of greenhorns were in charge of the drag. The cattle had slowed to a shuffling plod or stopped altogether.

Andi nudged Dusty into the muddle, where he went to work nipping the lag-behinds. They bellowed their annoyance and broke into a run. Andi loped over to Flint. "Mitch sent me to help."

Flint nodded his thanks. He looked ready to drop. "I've spurred and jerked my horse going after those slowpokes until I'm ashamed of myself."

In the distance, Levi yanked his horse after a dodging steer. His mount went one way; Levi went the other. He flew from his horse and crashed to the ground.

"Levi!" Visions of his tumble back on the ranch spurred Andi into action. She raced Dusty across the rangeland and flung herself from the saddle. "Are you hurt?"

Levi sat up clenching his fists. "I *hate* drag riding!" Tears pooled his bloodshot eyes. "I signed up for Cook's helper, not this. You know I'm no good rounding up cattle."

"You'll learn," Andi said. "And you'll be paid a man's wages for doing a man's job. Don't give up. Mitch is counting on you."

Levi paused, considering. He rubbed away his tears and took a deep, shuddering breath. "You're right." He staggered to his feet and climbed back on his horse. "Don't tell Uncle Mitch what I said."

Andi nodded. "So long as you promise not to tell Mitch how tired and miserable *I* am."

Levi thrust out his hand. "It's a deal."

CHAPTER 20

We're so shorthanded I think Mitch has forgotten he has a sister on this cattle drive. I also think he's forgotten I'm a girl. Or that Levi is a twelve-year-old boy punching cows. To Mitch, we're part of the crew, and he needs all the help he can get. I'm not sure I like being "just one of the hands."

Two days later Andi shaded her eyes and gazed at the mouth of the Grapevine, a steep, mountain canyon that left the flat San Joaquin Valley behind and ascended south through the Tehachapi range. Andi had never traveled these mountains before. She looked forward to the new scenery and to staying the night at the old Fort Tejon grounds.

Didn't Bryce say we might catch a glimpse of wandering camels at the fort? A fleeting sorrow pricked Andi's heart. She missed Bryce. She missed his tales. He would have enjoyed going on a "camel hunt" this afternoon after the cattle were settled.

Andi shook herself free of her musing and urged the *remuda* upwards. The mountains rose on both sides of the grade as the outfit climbed upward toward Tejon Pass. Unlike the high Sierra, no towering pines or sequoias grew on these slopes. Instead, the rolling hills lay covered in a carpet of new spring grass and wildflowers—orange, yellow, red, and purple—for as far as Andi could see.

"This is the best time of year to travel in these mountains," Mitch told her. "Plenty of water and lots of grass. Not to mention the privilege of seeing God's paintbrush on display."

"God's paintbrush," she said softly. "That's just what it is!"

Andi drank in the beauty of the surrounding landscape as she and Dusty urged the *remuda* farther into the mountains. The grade was steep but not impassable, and Mitch set a brisk, steady pace for the herd. They followed a well-established road, which made keeping the herd together much easier than driving them through the valley they'd recently left behind. The only fault Andi could find with using the road was all the dust the cattle churned up.

"I think the drive is getting a little easier," Andi told Dusty. "At least for me." She spent her days changing out horses for the drovers and caring for the used mounts. With Dusty along, the *remuda* gave her no trouble. She kept the horses well ahead of the cattle and the chuck wagon. "The only bad part is when I'm stuck giving Levi and Flint a hand." She rubbed her nose thinking about all that dust in her face, her hair, and her throat.

With permission from Mr. Beale, the ranch owner of this vast splendor, Cook set up camp at the old Fort Tejon grounds, a level expanse surrounded by steep hills, spreading oaks, and a year-round creek. The old adobe buildings didn't house soldiers anymore. Instead, livestock and ranch workers filled the extra spaces.

"Where do you suppose they keep the camels?" Andi joked to Cook after she'd watered the tired *remuda* at the creek and joined him and Rico late in the afternoon.

Cook cracked a smile. "The camels are no more, but I did see them in my youth," he confessed. "The young cowhand spoke the truth."

"Really? You never said anything."

"And ruin a good story?" Cook shook his head. "No, *chica*. I know when to hold my tongue." He chuckled and handed Andi the coffee grinder. "I could use your help, since you appear finished with the *remuda*. Rico is collecting firewood."

A finger of guilt tickled Andi's conscience. Thanks to knowing her way around horses—and with plenty of help from Dusty—she now had the easiest job of the outfit and more time on her hands than anybody else. She sat down in the shade with the grinder. As she worked, she heard woodpeckers, watched scrub jays swoop, and caught a glimpse high overhead of a condor soaring in the sapphire sky. She sighed. What a beautiful, restful spot.

Andi's peaceful rest lasted ten minutes. Mitch trotted into camp and didn't bother to dismount. "I need you and Dusty," he ordered.

Groaning inwardly, Andi set aside the grinder. "Is it more drag riding?" She tried to keep her voice cheerful for Mitch's sake, but a whine leaked out.

Mitch looked haggard, and more than a little frustrated. "What else?" he said wearily. "Going up that grade today put the tail end farther behind than ever. I want you to help the drag riders push those stragglers to catch up. They need time to graze this evening."

Andi rose with a shudder. An hour or two of riding behind the herd wore her out more than a full day of wrangling horses. *How many times will I have to keep doing this?* She stifled her silent wail. "Sure thing, boss."

"Good. I gotta get back." Mitch started to gallop away. Then he swiveled and brought his horse around. "I'm sorry, sis," he said.

"I can handle it." Andi straightened her shoulders. "Don't worry."

Mitch gave her a crooked smile and headed back to the herd, clearly confident his new wrangler would carry out his instructions.

Andi couldn't see the approaching herd, but she heard them mooing and bellowing just out of sight as they made their way up the final slope. By the time she saddled Dusty and loped toward the road, the long, dark line of steers stretched out downhill for as far as she could see.

They were hard to miss. Plodding along the narrow road, the cattle stirred up the dirt into a billowing cloud above them. She hurried along the line, waving to Kirby as she passed. A fit of sneezing convinced her to lift her bandana over her nose to block the worst of the dust. Her eyes watered but she pressed on.

Andi nudged Dusty into a faster gait. He responded with his usual breakneck gallop, and it wasn't long before the back end of the herd came into sight. Andi reined Dusty to a stop and lowered her bandana. She didn't need it any longer. These cattle were so far behind that the dust had settled.

"Oh, no!" Andi moaned. Three or four dozen steers were poking their way along the steep road following the main herd. A few just stood in the middle of the road, looking bored. At least a dozen cattle had broken away and were headed back toward the valley.

What a mess!

Andi shaded her eyes from the sun's glare. Flint circled the stragglers, desperately trying to move them faster but with little success. His horse acted skittish and looked done in. Farther down the road near the deserting cattle, Levi's horse sidestepped and twisted next to a third mount—a magnificent, white horse.

Andi caught her breath. What was Toledo doing riding drag? More importantly, why was he scuffling with Levi instead of rounding up the quickly disappearing steers?

Remembering Mitch's instructions, Andi left Flint to his own devices. At least he was moving his group of the cattle in the right direction. She kicked her heels into Dusty and headed for Toledo and Levi. "Maybe the three of us can turn those others around before they get too far," she muttered under her breath.

Andi hauled her horse to a dust-churning stop next to Sultan and Toledo. "Why aren't you two going after those—" She broke off, bewildered at the sight. Toledo had Levi's horse by the reins. His other hand gripped his knotted rope-end.

Andi's gaze shot to Levi, and her heart skipped. A bloody spot seeped through Levi's shirt sleeve. Tears streaked his dirty face. His eyes were two pools of terror mixed with helpless rage. He shook so hard he could barely keep his seat.

Wrath surged through Andi. "What are you *doing*? Let him go!"

Toledo dropped the reins. With one snap of his rope, he sent Levi's horse bolting. Andi whirled to follow, but she didn't get far. Toledo's arm snaked out and he snagged Dusty's reins. "Whoa there, little filly," he said. "You're in a mighty big hurry. What's the rush?"

"In case you haven't noticed, this part of the herd is scattering." She waved her hand toward the valley. "Why aren't you taking care of those steers? They're headed in the wrong direction."

"Nah." Toledo shrugged. "They're headed just where I want 'em to go."

The heat, the dust, and the shock of seeing Levi hurt and the steers scattered befuddled Andi. She couldn't make sense of Toledo's words. "What do you mean?" She glared at him. "Mitch sent me here to help round up the stragglers, and that's what I'm going to do."

"Really! I thought you were the wrangler." He chuckled.

Andi straightened in her saddle and yanked at the reins. They didn't budge. "You better get back to work. Get these steers headed in the right direction or Mitch will have your hide."

Toledo's eyebrows rose. "You're mighty bossy for a slip of a girl."

"*Shut up!*" Andi jerked at Dusty's reins again. "Let go of my horse," she ordered between clenched teeth. "I'll go after the cattle myself."

Toledo whistled, long and low. "You are *so* pretty when you've got your dander up, Miss Andi." He tossed aside his rope whip and swung down from Sultan. Before Andi could blink, he reached up and wrenched her from the saddle.

Andi's knees buckled. She stumbled to the ground. "What's wrong with you?" Shaking with anger, she leaped to her feet. "If you don't get back to work, Mitch will fire you."

Toledo clamped his hands down on Andi's shoulders and leaned closer. "I'll save him the trouble," he said in a low, silky voice. "I quit."

Andi's stomach turned over. Her threat of Mitch firing Toledo was just a bluff. "You c-can't quit," she stammered. "Mitch is shorthanded as it is."

"That's *his* problem." Toledo smirked. "I meant to part company with this outfit three days ago during the confusion at the river crossing." He shook his head. "Huey made it. I didn't."

Andi felt the blood drain from her face. So, Toledo *did* know the two drifters he'd met in the woods the other day, the ones who shot Chad and stole their beef! She swallowed the fury that rose up and threatened to consume her. "You dirty, double-crossing—"

"One thing went wrong," Toledo cut in. "You made off *with my horse*, leaving me afoot after pulling that wretched chuck wagon ashore. I had to wait for another opportunity. With the outfit so shorthanded, I knew I wouldn't have to wait long."

Andi gasped as the pieces fell into place. Toledo's anger at her for taking Sultan was not simply because she hadn't asked his permission. She'd kept him from getting away. She smiled inwardly. *Good.*

Toledo flicked his gaze in the direction of the steers headed downhill. "I'm taking those steers with me."

"Oh, no, you're not!" Andi shouted, trying to wriggle free.

Toledo's fingers dug into her shoulders. "Who's going to stop me? *You?* I'd already be long gone if that smart-aleck kid hadn't gotten in my way."

Andi tried to peer around Toledo. Where was Levi? She gave a sudden jerk and twisted free.

Before she'd gone three steps, Toledo caught her arm and yanked her back. "Not so fast, Miss Andi." His low chuckle sent prickles of fear racing up her spine. "Before I go, I intend to collect payment for your use of Sultan. I was disappointed when I thought I might miss my chance, but you arrived just in time."

Horror surged through Andi when Toledo bent close to kiss her. Quick as a striking rattlesnake, she curled her fist and slammed it into his face. Bull's-eye! Her knuckles burned, but she felt giddy with relief. It wasn't as if she didn't have experience clobbering a boy who stepped over the line.

Too late Andi realized Toledo was not like other boys she knew. He was nothing like Johnny Wilson, who'd covered his face and wailed at being punched by a girl. Toledo wasn't much older than Johnny, but hard work had matured him. His crushing grip showed Andi he'd barely reacted to her carefully aimed blow.

"That wasn't very nice," was all Toledo said before he tried again. This time he succeeded.

At Toledo's kiss, a storm rose in Andi that threatened to choke her. She couldn't breathe; she couldn't scream. But she *could* scratch and kick. Andi lit into him with all her strength. Her right boot connected with his shin. Toledo grunted but didn't let go. She raked her fingernails down his cheeks, but he seemed impervious to the pain.

Then suddenly, incredibly, Andi was free. She plummeted backward and hit the dirt with a painful *oof!* Sucking in huge gulps of air, she opened her mouth to scream. Nothing came out. From above, she heard a painful, enraged shriek.

Toledo was roaring like a wounded grizzly bear.

CHAPTER 21

I don't think I ever really appreciated Levi until today. I always thought a younger brother would be too much trouble. Now I wish Levi were my little brother. He's good to have around in a pinch.

Andi had no time to recover from the shock and disgust she'd felt at Toledo's touch. No time even to breathe a grateful prayer for her miraculous release. She scuttled, crablike, away from the crazy drover and tried to make sense of what had just happened.

Any second now, Andi expected Toledo to come after her and finish what he'd started. When he didn't, she rolled over and staggered to her feet, fighting her wobbly legs and the dizziness that threatened to flatten her. She forced herself to take slow, calming breaths. When Toledo bellowed again, she turned toward the commotion . . . and gasped.

Levi held the discarded, knotted rope-end in his hand and was lashing Toledo with it. He rained blows down against the man's arms, legs, and back as fast as he could snap the rope.

Toledo turned and lunged for Levi, but the boy was too quick. Between each stroke, Levi darted backward, dodged, and came up swinging. Toledo threw his full weight at Levi and tripped, crashing to the ground. Levi delivered more stinging blows then skipped out of the way.

"What's got into you, boy?" Toledo wheezed, rising to his feet. He looked genuinely puzzled. "What's wrong with a little kiss?"

"Andi doesn't want you to kiss her, *that's* what!" He danced clear of Toledo's long reach.

Toledo and Levi circled each other warily. Levi was panting; his chest heaved.

The drover narrowed his eyes. "How do you know what she wants? I've been told I'm a good kisser."

"Who told you that?" Levi taunted. *"Sultan?"* He turned tail and ran.

Toledo howled and gave chase. "I'll catch you, boy!" he thundered. "And when I do—"

A shower of gritty dirt in his face cut Toledo's threat short. Levi scooped up another handful and took off. But it looked like Toledo had recovered his wits. With long, swift strides, he bore down on the boy, closing the distance.

Levi's peril jolted Andi from her woozy state, clearing her mind faster than a thunderclap. Levi had lured Toledo away from her; now it was her turn to help her plucky nephew. She sprinted for Dusty. "Please, God," she prayed as she clambered into the saddle. "Make Dusty behave."

For once, Dusty didn't try any monkey business. Perhaps he sensed Andi's urgency, or maybe he was too surprised by his rider's speed in mounting to engage in his usual crow-hopping. Whatever the reason, the instant Dusty felt Andi's weight on his back he stretched out his neck and raced away. She thanked God and held on.

Worry for Levi snuffed out any fear she felt for her own safety. She gritted her teeth and barreled toward Toledo at full speed. She had no clear idea of what she'd do when she caught up. A fuzzy thought tickled her mind. Running him down seemed the only option to keep him from catching Levi. "With pleasure," she muttered.

Dusty clearly disagreed with Andi's trampling plans. At the last moment, he swerved to avoid the drover, clipping him soundly as he galloped past. Toledo went flying. He landed several yards away with a dull *thud* and lay still.

The impact nearly flung Andi from her saddle. She clung to Dusty's neck and righted herself. "Whoa there," she commanded, pulling back on the reins. Dusty tossed his head, snorted, and slowed to a nervous trot. She circled around. "Levi!" she called.

Levi stopped and whirled. Andi loped to meet him. Gasping, Levi grabbed a stirrup and collapsed against Dusty. Under the dirt and tears, his face was a sickly gray. He looked up at Andi with huge, red-rimmed eyes. "Are you"—he swallowed—"all right?"

"I'm fine on the outside," Andi said weakly. She brushed away a sudden splash of tears. "But I'm pretty shook up inside. What about you?"

"Ready to keel over." He shifted his hold on the stirrup and winced. "And I hurt. That skunk gave it to me pretty good. But I got him good too. At least enough to make him leave you alone." With his free hand, Levi lifted the knotted rope-end to Andi. "Here. Take it. I don't want it anymore." His fingers shook.

Andi took the makeshift whip gingerly. Her throat tightened. Earlier, this nasty piece of rope had sent Levi's horse bolting. What might have happened to her if Levi hadn't returned and had the wit to find it and use it on Toledo? "You . . . you saved me," she whispered.

"Well, you saved me from drowning the other day," Levi said with a glimmer of his usual self. "Now we're even."

Andi's heart overflowed with gratitude for her daring nephew. The rough edges he'd acquired from growing up with a scoundrel for a father had served him well today. Levi had lit into Toledo without considering the risks to himself. "Toledo could have hurt you badly."

Levi shrugged. "I know." He cracked a grin. "That's why I was running."

A loud groan brought them both around. Twenty yards away, Toledo had come to. Andi's stomach turned over when she saw him rise groggily to his knees. His fancy shirt was torn, revealing a series of bloody marks— Levi's doing. He hunched over, his hands on his knees, swaying slightly.

Andi reached out to Levi. "Let's get out of here. Mitch needs to know what Toledo's up to, and those steers are heading farther downhill by the minute. We can't let Toledo make off with them."

"Oh yes we can," Levi said. "I'm not going after them." He took Andi's hand and scrambled up behind her. "My horse wandered off. He's over there." He pointed to a low rise covered with wildflowers some distance from the road. Sultan grazed next to Levi's bay.

Andi fingered the knotted rope and chewed her lip in thought. Sultan was a gorgeous animal. A pity he belonged to a scoundrel like Toledo. The stallion deserved better. "What should we do about his horse?" she asked.

Levi snorted. "We sure can't leave him here. I say we wallop him with the rope and leave Toledo afoot."

Andi pondered. "What if Sultan comes back? Maybe we should take him to Mitch and let him decide what to do."

"Whatever we do, we better do it quick. Toledo's coming to his senses." Panic edged Levi's voice.

Andi tossed the rope aside and chirruped to Dusty. A steady lope brought the two of them next to the horses in no time. Andi waited until Levi mounted his horse. Then she circled Sultan and pulled up beside his head.

"Easy, boy," she murmured. "You're coming with us."

A sharp whistle pierced the air just as Andi reached for Sultan's reins. The stallion's head snapped up and his ears pricked forward. Then he reared and gave an answering whinny. A second later, he slammed his hooves into the ground and dashed away, brushing so close to Andi that she could feel his hot breath. His mane whipped across her face.

Andi sidestepped Dusty out of the way. Close call! If she had hold of Sultan's reins, she'd have surely been yanked from the saddle and trampled. Catching her breath, she watched the horse gallop toward his master. Whatever else Toledo was, he was a good judge of horseflesh. Sultan could easily match any Circle C horse for intelligence, stamina, and beauty.

Levi brought Andi back to the here and now. "Let's *go!* Before Toledo comes after us."

"He won't," Andi said, shaking her head. "Not now. He won't take the time."

Toledo had clearly lost this round. Andi was sure he'd round up the dozen or so steers he'd cut out earlier and continue his way back into the San Joaquin Valley. He'd meet up with Huey and those other two, and they'd have themselves a nice little herd to sell. There were plenty of unscrupulous buyers willing to close their eyes to the Circle C brand mark in exchange for a good price on the beef.

In the distance, Toledo limped to Sultan and mounted. He turned toward them, but instead of closing the distance he lifted his hat in good-bye and headed down the road.

Andi's stomach roiled at his smug farewell. Her ire rose, and she embraced it. Anger kept the adrenaline flooding her bloodstream; it kept her from crumpling into a blubbering, swooning heap. Anger kept her encounter with Toledo tucked away in a corner of her mind to work through later.

Right now, Mitch needed to know about this double-crossing rider. And *soon*, before Toledo got away with more Carter beef. She dug her heels into Dusty and took off toward their camp at Fort Tejon, with Levi mere hoofbeats behind.

CHAPTER 22

I need to be more careful what I wish for.
Sometimes I get it.

Andi and Levi charged past the grazing herd on lathered horses. The cattle were spread out in quiet, contented clumps under the shade of the oak trees that dotted the fort's expansive grounds. At the riders' approach, a number of steers lumbered to their feet in alarm; they settled down once the threat to their peace had passed.

Flint was just bringing in his stragglers. "Where have you two been?" he hollered. "I had to fight these . . ."

His words buzzed in Andi's ear as she raced by. Before Dusty came to a full stop, she slid from the saddle and ran helter-skelter through camp, screaming for Mitch. Wyatt and two other drovers lounged around the campfire, sipping coffee. At Andi's shriek, they sprang to their feet. Hot coffee splattered everywhere.

"What's all the hullabaloo?" Wyatt demanded, wiping coffee from the leather chaps protecting his trousers. "I barely sat down for a moment's rest, and you scared a year's growth outta me. Next, you'll be stampeding the herd." He scowled.

Andi streaked past the men. Her throat was too clogged with tears to speak normally, and her heart hammered out of control. "Mitch!" she wailed.

Young Rico stood stock-still, his arms full of firewood. He gaped at

Andi like she was *loco*. Cook planted his fists on his hips. *"¿Qué pasó, chica?"*

Andi didn't answer. She whirled, ducked around the chuck wagon, and collided with Mitch's chest, knocking the breath out of her. She coughed and stumbled backward.

"Hey, sis, take it easy." Mitch steadied her and led her back to the fire. "Did you bring in the stragglers like I asked?"

Andi shook her head. She found a spot on the log and pulled Mitch down beside her. She clutched his vest like a lifeline. Her words tumbled out, one on top of the other.

Mitch's face darkened at the recital.

"You *have* to go after him," Andi finished. "Toledo's driving our steers down the grade *right now*. He—"

"She didn't tell you the rest of it," Levi broke in. He helped himself to a handful of raisins and plopped to the ground. His eyes flashed. Before Andi could stop him, he gave a full account of Toledo's churlish behavior toward her.

The men exploded into an uproar. "That does it, boss!" Wyatt growled. He waved his good arm toward the grade. "We won't stand for that no-good cockerel manhandling our Miss Andi."

"This is an affront to the *señorita's* honor," Cook said darkly in Spanish.

"You must pass out the six-shooters, *señor*, and go after Toledo," Diego insisted. His eyes narrowed to two dark slits. "For many reasons, not the least to bring the cattle back."

Murmurs of agreement echoed the Mexican cowhand's suggestion.

Andi ducked her head. A warm glow replaced her trembling. The men's loyalty went a long way toward dispelling the horrible vision that kept replaying itself in her head. The knots in her stomach began to untangle.

Mitch said nothing. He put a consoling arm around Andi and nestled her close. He gave no outward sign, but his silence and his clenched jaw spoke volumes—he was holding back simmering rage.

The men downed what remained of their coffee and stood up. "What're we waitin' for?" Kirby said. "Let's go after the sidewinder."

"I'll round up the rest of the men," Wyatt added. "We'll settle this quick enough."

Mitch didn't budge. He sat like a stone, staring into the fire. A muscle in his jaw twitched.

"Boss?"

"No."

Loud protests erupted. The drovers all started talking at once. Flint joined the group and added his two-cents' worth when he heard what the ruckus was all about.

Mitch closed his eyes. Andi knew he was praying for wisdom. He needed it. This cattle drive was unraveling at lightning speed. With Toledo gone, they were now down another man. And several days' travel through the mountains still awaited them.

Mitch opened his eyes and waited for the commotion to die down. One by one, the drovers quieted and resumed their positions around the fire.

"That's better." Mitch took a deep breath and looked around at the angry faces. "I see five able-bodied men sitting here; three more are out with the herd. I can't risk leaving those steers unguarded while we chase after Toledo."

"We oughta do *somethin'*," Kirby argued. "Huey and his cohorts plugged Chad and made off with eighty head. Toledo insulted your sister and stole a dozen more. That's a whole bunch o' slurs against this outfit, not to mention almost a hundred less cattle not going to market."

Andi added it up in her head. One hundred steers times forty dollars was . . . "That's four thousand dollars, Mitch!"

"I know how much it is." He turned to Kirby. "We're going to do something, you can be sure of that. *We're going to drive the rest of these cattle to Los Angeles.* Evening's coming on, and I need every man jack of you to guard the cattle we still have—not waste what little energy you have left chasing Toledo in the dark." His gaze turned hard. "If you think you won't get paid because we're short some beef, don't worry. You'll get paid."

"You're going to let Toledo go?" Levi squeaked.

Mitch nodded.

Wyatt snorted. "If Chad was here, he'd—"

"*I'm* bossing this drive, Wyatt," Mitch snapped. He shot to his feet so fast Andi found herself on the ground. "*I* give the orders. Not Chad. Not you. Is that clear?"

A deathly hush fell over the camp. Mitch stood facing down his vengeance-happy men. A minute went by. Then two.

Finally, Wyatt backed down. "I'm sorry, boss. I meant no disrespect. It just riles me to let that skunk get away with this." He slumped and held his head in his good hand, clearly exhausted.

Mitch relaxed. He sat down again. "I don't like it any better than you do, Wyatt. But the few cattle Toledo took aren't worth wearing ourselves out for. We still have a long ways to go. Knowing Andi and Levi are safe is what's important."

Grunts of agreement rippled through the group. The men settled down. "I'm bushed," Kirby said. He lay back and closed his eyes. "Hope I'm not up for night duty right away." He tugged his hat over his forehead and instantly began snoring.

The rich odor of simmering stew and hot biscuits drifted over Andi. She peeked behind her shoulder. Cook stood busying himself with a fire of his own. When he caught Andi looking at him, he winked.

Wily old Cook! Andi thought. A hot, filling meal and plenty of coffee would calm the men even better than Mitch's words. A minute later Rico ran a big spoon around the inside of the metal triangle, calling the hands for supper.

The somber group ate in shifts. Those not eating or on guard duty slept. No one had the energy or interest to sit around the fire and swap tall tales. Andi fell asleep the moment her head touched her saddle.

What felt like a minute later, somebody was shaking her awake. "Huh?" She sat up with a start.

Mitch knelt beside her. "Remember that night a while back when you wished you could go on night duty but I wouldn't let you?"

Andi looked at him blankly. Being awakened in the middle of the night did not help her memory. She nodded anyway. If Mitch remembered her asking to do it, it must be true. She rubbed her eyes and yawned.

"Well, I need a partner tonight so the rest of the outfit can sleep. It's two o'clock. You'll take the last shift with me." Mitch rose and pulled Andi to her feet. "Only, don't tell Mother. She'll have my hide."

There was no moon, but thousands of stars hung low in the sky, giving the night a pale, silvery look. Andi stumbled around in the gloom to find Dusty, who acted bad-tempered at being forced to work in the middle of the night. Mitch tried to saddle him, but the horse behaved so badly he sent Andi back to the *remuda* for a different mount.

Instead of the usual three night guards, Mitch had downsized to two. In this peaceful, protected area of the Tehachapi Mountains, the cattle quieted right away. A good thing too. Andi had no intention of singing any *yippee-yi-yay* songs to a bunch of cows.

Plodding around and around the herd, the first hour dragged; the second hour stopped altogether. So did Andi's horse, especially when she caught herself nodding off in the saddle. She started awake twice, and Mitch nudged her out of drowsing three more times.

Andi nearly wept when a pale streak of dawn colored the eastern sky above the range. "Oh, please, God," she prayed. "I don't ever want to ride night guard again." She heard a clip-clopping from behind and shifted in her saddle.

Mitch trotted up with a steaming mug of coffee. He handed it to Andi. "This'll wake you up. Cook's rustling around the campsite, and Rico made coffee."

"Thanks." Andi greedily sipped the strong brew. She slowly felt herself reviving to face the new day.

Together, brother and sister watched the dawn grow brighter. "I'm sorry for what happened yesterday with Toledo," Mitch said after a few minutes. "I've been kicking myself for forgetting who you are and treating you like one of my cowhands. I should have never let you out of my sight—or Cook's."

"But you needed my help," Andi reminded him.

"Not *that* badly. From now on you'll stick to wrangling the horses—up where Cook can see you. I won't send you back with Flint and Levi, no matter how desperate I get for good help."

Andi nodded, relieved. Riding drag was a sorry business. "I want to apologize again for not telling you about those two drifters Levi and I—"

Mitch cut her off with a shake of his head. "I told you that's over."

"No, there's more," Andi said, swallowing. "Levi and I saw Toledo heading for the smoke of their campsite that day. When I asked what he was doing, he gave me a story about finding out the drifters' business. He said he'd tell you." She hung her head. "I believed him and let it go. He . . . he fooled me."

"That's not all he did," Mitch said between gritted teeth. "He'd better hope I never find him."

"Everything's gone wrong," Andi said. Tears pooled in her eyes. "I'm sorry."

"None of this is your fault." Mitch reached across their horses and cupped Andi's face in his gloved hands. "Do you hear me, little sister? Cattle rustling is just one of the hazards of a trail drive, along with river crossings, bad weather, scarce water, and lousy fodder. Be glad we don't have to worry about Indians, like the outfits trailing the Great Plains. I think we've done all right."

Mitch let her go and lifted his reins. "The people I care about most are safe. Even shorthanded, we'll make it to Los Angeles in one piece. I promise." He scanned the horizon and nodded. "Drink up. The day's a'wastin'."

CHAPTER 23

I'm not one bit sorry this cattle drive is over. I am sorry, though, that we have two more days of traveling left to endure before I'm finally home. Mitch says two days by train is better than another week or two going home by stagecoach. He's right.

Mitch kept his promise. For several days they drove the herd over passes, into canyons, up steep grades, through more passes, and then down a steep descent into the San Fernando Valley. Everyone was bleary-eyed from serving double duty, but no more crises hounded their route.

After nearly three weeks on the trail, Andi was dog-tired, and starved for the amenities she'd always taken for granted at home: a soft bed, a sit-down meal, and—most importantly—a real bath. Dirt was her second skin now. She hadn't had a thorough washing since nearly drowning in the Kern River twelve days ago.

Andi and Levi stood at the top of Cahuenga Pass in the Santa Monica Mountains the morning of their last day out and gazed south. A small city lay nestled in the basin below. Andi had never seen anything so beautiful. Los Angeles didn't appear very large, and she saw nothing special that made it stand out, but to her comfort-starved eyes it truly looked like the "city of angels."

"I can't wait to get there," she said with a sigh of longing.

"You and me both," Levi agreed. He and Flint had finally caught on to the skill of riding the drag. They'd poked and prodded the rear of the herd into keeping up, and Mitch praised them for their work. But Levi had paid a heavy price for his new ability to herd cattle. Dark circles rimmed his eyes, and he looked twice as filthy as Andi. "If Mama saw me now, she'd have a conniption fit."

"If Mother saw *me*, she'd probably have a fit right along with Kate." Andi poked Levi and grinned. "After all, we were supposed to be Cook's helpers, not a wrangler and a cowpuncher."

Rico joined them. His dark eyes gleamed when he saw the city. *"El Pueblo de la Reina de Los Angeles."*

Andi rolled her eyes and translated the city's outlandish name for Levi. "The Town of the Queen of Angels." Then she laughed. "Are you kidding us, Rico?" she asked in Spanish.

"No," Rico insisted. *"¡Es la verdad!"*

It *was* true. The little boy knew a lot about the town on the banks of the beautiful river sparkling in the distance. When he told Andi the river's name, she laughed harder.

"What's he saying?" Levi demanded.

Andi pointed to the river. "It's called 'Our Lady of the Angels of the Little Portion,' but don't ask me why anybody would—"

"It's the Los Angeles River," Mitch said, coming up behind his three youngest trail hands. "Let's just leave it at that for now." He gave Levi a slap on the seat of his pants. Dust flew. "You've done all right for your first time punching cows, partner. Ready for the last ten miles?"

Levi drew a deep breath. "Sure thing, Uncle Mitch." But it didn't sound like his heart was in it.

Neither was Andi's. She heaved a sigh and climbed into her saddle to wrangle the *remuda* one last time.

By late afternoon, the cattle were counted and gathered into the stockyard in a noisy, bawling jumble. When Mitch closed the gate behind the last balky steer and latched it, he slapped the dust from his gloved hands and slumped against the railings. "Thank God," he murmured.

"For a 'short' trip, this sure was a twister," Wyatt said. His sprained wrist hung in a dirty, makeshift sling. "Let the army get their beef from a closer source next time. I'd rather drive cattle north to Stockton."

Mitch agreed. "The army offered top dollar, but I'm not sure it was worth it. They're not even getting the full thousand." He shook his head. "The final count came in at nine hundred three."

Major Gordon met Mitch at the stockyard. "You're a couple of days late," he chided. "But the steers look good. I can tell you didn't push 'em hard. Too bad it's not the full quota, but it's close enough." He grunted his satisfaction and paid Mitch the agreed-upon price per head.

"I wouldn't get top dollar if I brought in trail-worn steers," Mitch said as he and the major shook hands. He didn't elaborate on the reasons he'd missed the army's deadline, or why he was nearly a hundred steers short.

He probably doesn't think the details of a cattle drive are any of the army's business, Andi thought. *So long as they get their beef.* She and Levi trailed along behind Mitch when they finally left the tumult of the stockyard. "When can we get cleaned up?" she asked.

"Not yet." Mitch led the way to the bank, deposited thousands of dollars, and paid off the temporary crew with the money he kept out. He thanked Kirby, Tripp, and Seth and sent them on their way. They yelled their *yippee-yi-yays* and disappeared toward the center of town.

Andi had a feeling their money would soon be spent on new clothes, frivolous doodads, and in the saloons. A twinge of sadness that Bryce was not with them pinched Andi's heart.

The outfit had parted company with the chuck wagon just after noon, well before sending the cattle streaming into the stockyard. Cook and Rico had kinfolk in Los Angeles. The old man wanted to visit before seeing his nephew safely back to Bakersfield and returning to the ranch. He'd take the chuck wagon home in his own good time.

Andi shaded her eyes. The sun was quickly dipping toward the western horizon. The only loose end was the *remuda*. Mitch turned the horses over to the Circle C's regular hands with instructions to drive them slow and easy back to the ranch. "Take a few days off," he said when he handed over money for expenses. "You've earned it."

The four cowhands grinned their thanks.

Soon, Mitch, Andi, and Levi were free.

"Not a moment too soon," Andi muttered out of Mitch's hearing. She was sick of dirty, noisy cattle, and she itched all over. Her cheeks flamed when she stepped into the mercantile to buy clean clothes and a nightdress.

The proprietor arched his eyebrows at Andi's appearance but accepted her money. After all, she paid cash. He tied up her purchases in brown paper and shoved them across the counter with his fingertips. "Thank you . . . *ma'am*." He looked unconvinced that a young lady lay hidden beneath all that dirt.

Mitch and Levi gave Andi first dibs on the hotel's bathing room. She soaked in the tub until every finger and toe shriveled up like prunes. Mitch banged on the door twice, but Andi didn't get serious about finishing her bath until Levi threatened to barge in. Knowing Levi's rascally ways, she finished scrubbing in a hurry.

The best surprise came after supper when Andi stepped into her hotel room. Mitch had paid extra so she wouldn't have to share the bed with a snoring old lady or another woman stranger. Andi stretched out under the fresh, clean sheets and sighed in pure pleasure.

She didn't savor this luxury for long, however. She fell asleep too fast.

—·—

"Andi." Mitch's whisper and a slight bouncing on the mattress jarred Andi awake. It was still dark.

"Huh?" she mumbled groggily.

"The train to Bakersfield leaves in half an hour."

"Uh-huh." She rolled over.

Mitch shook her. "Meet Levi and me in front of the hotel in fifteen minutes or I'll leave you behind."

It was on the tip of Andi's tongue to tell Mitch to leave her behind. The bed was soft, and she was *so* tired. Then her eyes popped open and she threw the covers aside. "We're meeting Chad in Bakersfield!"

"Yep." Mitch slipped from the room.

Fifteen minutes later Andi was dressed in the new clothes she'd purchased the day before. A sloppy but clean braid trailed down her back. She held a cheap carpetbag, in which she'd stuffed her trail clothes, work boots, and hat—dirt and all. "I'm ready," she told Mitch when she met him and Levi on the hotel's veranda.

Mitch nodded. He handed her a bread-and-butter sandwich to tide her over and hurried them toward the railroad depot in the predawn. Andi gobbled her breakfast on the run.

No sooner had Andi boarded the train and plopped down beside Mitch on the red-velvet bench seat than her eyelids drooped. Levi's nose stayed glued to the window, but Andi didn't care about the scenery. The rocking, swaying car put her to sleep faster than the conductor could holler, "All aboard!"

The next thing Andi knew, the whistle blew and the train's wheels squealed to a stop in Bakersfield. Mitch shoved her head upright, off his shoulder. "You slept all morning," he said. "You didn't even twitch when we picked up passengers in Mojave."

"And you missed the Loop," Levi told her, his eyes full of awe. "The railroad track passes over itself in a big circle as it climbs higher. I never saw such a sight!"

Andi shrugged. Feeling refreshed after her long nap was worth missing one of the engineering wonders of the railroad world.

Chad met them at the station, all smiles. "Howdy, little sister," he called. "You look clean for once, and a real pretty sight for sore eyes."

Andi's heart swelled to see Chad standing straight and tall, clean-shaven and dressed in a new shirt and denim britches. "And you look *alive*," she bantered back. "Much better than the last time I saw you." She tapped his left side. "Is there a bandage tucked under your shirt, holding you together?"

Chad flinched at her touch and brushed her hand away. "All right, so I'm not one hundred percent yet." He picked up Andi's satchel with the hand on his good side and fell into step beside Mitch. "The train to Fresno leaves tomorrow morning at seven. I've arranged for you to stay at Mrs. Stewart's boardinghouse, where I've been laid up for the past twelve *long* days."

"Been counting the days, have you?" Mitch chuckled.

Chad rolled his eyes. "I was never so happy to see a telegram than when yours came yesterday." His voice dropped. "Mrs. Stewart wouldn't let me out of the house until today, and that quack of a doctor backed her up." He grinned suddenly. "But she sure can cook. She's making chicken pie for supper."

"What about *dinner*?" Levi burst out a second before Andi.

"Yes, what about it?" she echoed Levi's question. "I had a scanty break-fast, and it's way past noon." She didn't mention that her stomach clam-ored to be filled with something besides beans and biscuits.

"The noon meal's long past here," Chad said. He led them up the boardinghouse's front porch and stepped inside. "But you can get some-thing to eat at the Two-Bit Café. It's just down the street. You and Levi go on ahead and find us a table. Order something. Mitch and I'll dump the bags and be right along."

Andi eagerly agreed. She thrust her hand into her skirt pocket and fingered the change from her shopping trip yesterday. If Mitch and Chad were delayed, she wanted to show the café's proprietor that she could pay. "Come on, Levi. I'm starved."

Andi clattered down the porch steps. She felt light and free and—for once—wide awake. Instead of keeping the *remuda* together, she was strolling down the streets of a lively little town. Bakersfield might not be as big as Fresno, but it was clean and bright. Colorful awnings shaded the boardwalk and fluttered in the breeze.

"There's the café across the street," Levi said when they'd gone two blocks.

Andi clasped Levi's hand and together they dodged the horse and wagon traffic. Before going inside, she stopped to read the sign in the café's window: "Lowest Prices in the Valley. Every Menu Item Under Two Bits."

Andi smiled. She had more cash in her pocket than a measly twenty-five cents. She could get a generous meal and a piece of pie besides. The aroma of fresh bread and fruit cobblers drifted through the café's screen door and set her mouth to watering. She yanked the door open and stepped inside. Levi scurried after her.

A dozen tables with red-checked tablecloths and wooden chairs were scattered around the room. Four or five held diners lingering over a late lunch. Andi picked out an empty table and started toward it. "Mitch and Chad won't have any trouble spotting us at this one."

Levi didn't reply. He plucked at Andi's sleeve. "See those men at the corner table?" he hissed in her ear. "They look mighty familiar."

Andi followed Levi's gaze to the corner of the café, where three men sat around a table, boisterously eating and drinking. One man sported a dark, handlebar mustache; another's black hair curled over his collar. The third man sat with his back to Andi, but it didn't take much work to guess it was Huey.

Andi's heart surged to her throat then settled in her chest with a painful throb. *The men who shot Chad. They're here. In Bakersfield!*

CHAPTER 24

Just when I thought my troubles were over . . .

"What'll we do?" Levi whispered. He eyed the men in the corner. "Do we sit down and wait for Chad and Mitch like nothing's wrong?"

Andi shook her head. "The minute Chad walks in they'll recognize him. And"—she swallowed hard—"they're wearing six-shooters. Let's go find the boys. They'll get the sheriff to arrest these thieves. Hurry. Before they—"

"May I seat you?"

Andi whirled and nearly plowed into a smiling, white-aproned waitress. "N-no, ma'am. I . . . we're waiting for my brothers." She grabbed Levi's hand and tugged. "We'll wait outside. Thank you." Her words tumbled out in a rush.

"As you like." The waitress nodded and returned to the kitchen.

Half a dozen quick steps took Andi and Levi to the open doorway. She glanced over her shoulder and let out a pleased breath. Nobody in the café showed any interest in their coming or going, least of all the men lounging at the out-of-the-way corner table.

Andi brought her attention around, pushed open the screen door . . . and froze. "Oh, no." She skipped backward, lurching into Levi. Before he could yelp, she clamped down on his arm and hauled him out of the doorway. "We're in trouble."

Toledo had just crossed the street and was stepping up onto the board-walk, headed straight for the café. If Andi walked through the door she would bump into him. She broke out in a cold sweat at the thought of being anywhere near the former drover.

Levi sucked in a startled breath and ducked behind the door.

Andi scanned the café for another way out. She spied a side door just past the corner table and edged her way toward it. But a better idea whispered in her head. *Find the proprietor, or even the waitress.* Toledo wouldn't dare try anything in broad daylight. Not in a crowded café.

She was wrong. Before she'd taken another step, Andi felt her left arm wrenched up behind her back until she gasped in pain.

"Don't scream," Toledo whispered in her ear. "Or I'll break your arm." He shoved it higher to show his sincerity. Andi winced. "Act like you know me. Quickly now." In a louder voice he said, "Well, what a surprise meeting you here, Miss Carter. How are you?"

Scared to death! Andi wanted to shriek. She glanced at Levi. He was untouched, but he'd obviously heard every word Toledo had whispered, for he stared at the concealed, viselike grip Toledo had on Andi. "I'm hungry, Mr. McGuire," Andi said in what she hoped was a normal voice. "Care to join me for lunch?"

At her words, the diners who had shown a brief interest in the disturbance returned to their half-eaten meals. Conversation resumed. Knives and forks clinked against dinner plates.

"Nicely done," Toledo said softly. He guided Andi toward the side door. "Now, come along. You too, boy." He passed the corner table and lowered his voice to his companions. "Let's go."

The men rose instantly. Looking grim, they tossed coins on the table and followed Toledo, Andi, and Levi outside. Once in the narrow alley, Toledo released Andi from the painful lock he had on her. But before she could run, he snaked one arm around her waist and clamped his hand over her mouth. "Scream all you want now, little lady."

Andi felt faint. Black spots exploded in front of her eyes. She tried to peel Toledo's fingers from her face but he was too strong. She shook her head to clear the dizziness and huffed air through flared nostrils.

A few feet away, the mustached man held Levi. His hand muffled the wildcat noises coming from his captive's mouth. Levi's face turned beet-red. He kicked and thrashed and pulled the cowhand's hair. Huey stepped in and delivered a blow that settled Levi down in a hurry. He moaned.

"This is just great," Huey growled. "I *told* you we were cutting it too close by staying in town this long. We shoulda got outta Bakersfield days ago, the minute we found a buyer for that beef. Now it won't be long till—"

"Carter's been here the whole time," Toledo said. "We've managed to stay out of his way."

"He's been laid up at the boardinghouse," Huey reminded him. "Not running around the streets like these two." He waved a hand at Andi. "She'll tell her brothers we're here and then . . ." He made a slicing motion across his neck. "We're done for."

"Not if we get rid of them," the dark-haired man put in.

"Uh-uh, Roy," Toledo protested. "I'll go along with taking the beef, but I stop short of killing anybody . . . especially young, pretty girls." His hold around Andi's middle tightened. "You sure cleaned up nice," he whispered.

Andi's empty stomach lurched. *I'm going to be sick.* She gagged and choked. Toledo loosened his hand from her mouth just enough so she could heave in a deep breath. It kept her from losing what little breakfast she'd eaten this morning.

"I say we stash 'em somewhere long enough to clear outta town," Huey said. "And we better do it before somebody comes lookin' for 'em." He glanced around nervously. "There. Brazo's livery is right around the corner." He pointed. "The old man's practically deaf and crippled. Let's gag these two, tie 'em up, and lock 'em in an unused stall. By the time Brazo finds 'em, we'll be across the river and clean away."

Toledo nodded amid grunts of agreement from the others. He relaxed his grip on Andi. "I'd never hurt you, you know," he told her softly. "I was only bluffing about breaking your arm." He grinned. "And it worked."

Andi stiffened. She didn't believe him for a second. Toledo's crazy moods popped up more unexpectedly than a jack-in-the-box. *A loose cannon*, she remembered her brothers saying.

Completely loco, Andi decided.

The four men quickly put their plan into action. One of them lifted Levi under his arms and one grabbed his legs before hurrying toward the back of the livery stable. Toledo and Huey followed suit with Andi, who slumped like deadweight.

Just before they reached the livery, Andi came to life. She kicked out her foot, catching Huey just under the chin. A satisfying *crunch* told her she'd struck her target.

Huey dropped Andi's other leg and clutched his jaw. "Augh!" He staggered backward then flew at Andi with both fists. One-handed, Toledo deflected the blows and thrust him aside. "Cut it out, Huey. You'll live."

In the confusion, Andi wriggled away from Toledo. But only for a second. He snatched her braid and hauled her back. "Not so fast."

A few minutes later it was all over. While Huey slumped on the ground near the building's back opening, groaning in pain, the other three found rags and ropes to secure their prisoners. They worked quickly and quietly so as to not arouse suspicion from the business end of the large livery stable. Mr. Brazo might be hard of hearing, but even he couldn't miss the noise if they banged around too loudly.

Toledo tightened the last knot in the rope that pinned Andi's wrists behind her back. He propped her against the wall and squatted in the hay next to her. "I'm sure sorry I can't finish that kiss," he said, stuffing a rag in her mouth. "But I'm afraid I've no time to do a proper job of it." He patted her cheek, rose, and tipped his hat. "It's been a pleasure, Miss Carter," he mocked then slipped out of the stall. The others trailed after him.

Andi heard the latch click, locking the two halves of the stall's door in place. Then silence. Tears threatened to flood her eyes, but she blinked them back. *No crying!* she ordered silently. Across from her, propped against the other wall, Levi started sniffling. She shook her head and glared at him. *No crying!*

Think, Andi Carter, she told herself. *Think how to get out of this fix.* She couldn't wait for the near-deaf Brazo to hobble to their rescue. Like Huey suggested, it could be hours—maybe the rest of the day and all night—before the livery owner checked on these stalls. She shivered. It was gloomy enough in here without darkness falling.

Andi looked around. A narrow window was cut into the outer wall near the rafters. No way out there. The stall's walls were sturdy planks, with only slim cracks between the slats. She crouched and pressed an eye against a slit. She couldn't see a thing in the darkened stall next door.

The ropes began to cut off Andi's circulation. Her hands burned. Tingles raced through her wrists. She flopped onto the scratchy hay and wriggled, wormlike, over to Levi. The least they could do was pull away these horrible gags. She needed a deep breath before she passed out.

Levi caught on to her idea and lowered his body within reach of Andi's bound hands. Wiggling her fingers, she felt behind her back for his gag. *Oops!* she thought when he groaned. That was his eye. Inch by inch, she walked her fingers down his face until she felt the rag. Then she yanked.

Levi gasped and drew in breath after breath. Then he returned the favor by removing Andi's gag. Wasting no time, they began to holler and scream. Andi scooted her way to the Dutch door and lay on her back. She didn't care how unladylike it was or how many petticoats and bloomers might show. She raised her legs and slammed her heels against the door using her bound ankles. Levi soon joined her.

Banging, hollering, resting, listening. The cycle went on for over an hour. "Maybe it's an abandoned livery stable," Levi said, panting. His foot-slamming had tapered off and his voice sounded hoarse. "We're making enough noise to wake snakes."

"No," Andi said. Her throat stung. "Listen. I hear the horses. I think we've unsettled them." A shrill whinny pierced her ears. She grinned.

"Yes, indeed. The horses are not happy. If nothing else, their complaining will bring somebody to investigate. Let's keep kicking at the door."

Another ten minutes of heel-banging passed until Andi's legs felt like jelly. The horses' whinnies grew louder. It sounded like every stabled horse in the livery had taken up the pattern. Hooves beat against stall doors up and down the aisle.

Then the sweetest sound Andi thought she would ever hear clicked in her ears. The latch pulled back. The top half of the stall door swung open. A grizzled faced peered down at them. The old man's eyes widened, but his voice was matter-of-fact.

"What're you doin' battering at my livery and frightening my horses?"

CHAPTER 25

When I read over my entries for the past three weeks, I marvel. Instead of mourning our losses and all the things that went wrong, I rejoice that so many things went right. The drive opened my eyes and cured me of my naïveté. Mitch says I showed my mettle and stuck it out. But I think I'll stay on the ranch from now on. Trail-driving is a risky, dangerous business.

Mr. Brazo cut Andi's and Levi's bonds, all the while muttering oaths about rowdies trespassing on his property and creating an uproar with their antics. Andi wasn't sure if he meant their captors or Levi and her. She shouted an explanation at the nearly deaf man, but he shook his head.

"Get outta here!" He shoved them down the wide passageway toward the front of the building. "If I catch you anywhere near my place again, I'll sic the sheriff on you."

The late afternoon sun nearly blinded Andi as she and Levi stumbled out of the livery stable and into the street. She brushed straw from her clothes and took off running toward the boardinghouse. Barging through the door, she screamed, "Chad! Mitch!"

Five or six boarders converged on her and Levi, including Mrs. Stewart, the proprietress. "Land sakes, child!" she exclaimed. "Your brothers are scouring the streets for you two. I've never seen such a to-do."

Footsteps thundered on the porch, and the screen door slammed.

"*Where have you been?*" Chad took Andi's shoulders and gave her a shake. "Of all the—"

"No time!" Andi yelled. "Toledo and the others are here." She poured out her story. Levi filled in the gaps.

Chad didn't waste a second. "Mrs. Stewart," he said in a quieter voice. "Please keep my sister and my nephew here. Give them something to eat. They've been through a lot. I'll find Mitch and let him know what's happening."

The plump, gray-haired woman smiled grimly. "Don't you worry, Mr. Carter. I'll see to their welfare. You and your brother make sure the sheriff catches up to those no-good cattle thieves." She gave Chad a motherly scowl. "Just don't go tearing open your injury, you hear me?"

"Yes, *ma'am*," Chad said. He plunked his hat on his head and raced out the door.

———

Levi had fallen asleep upstairs hours ago, but Andi waited on tenterhooks in the boardinghouse parlor for her brothers' return. When she heard boots clomping up the wooden porch steps and the door squeaking open, she sprang from her seat.

Their weary but satisfied smiles told Andi all she needed to know.

"Not only did we catch them," Mitch said, "but we also recovered the cash from our stolen beef. All four thieves are settled in the Bakersfield jail, awaiting a speedy trial." He slung an arm around Andi's shoulder and bent close to her ear. "Toledo resisted arrest. It was pure pleasure convincing him to come along quietly."

Andi couldn't help laughing. Her terrifying encounter with the former drover evaporated from her spirit like water on a hot day. "Thanks, Mitch," she whispered back.

Once again, the night was too short for Andi. Still yawning, she boarded the train to Fresno first thing in the morning, only half-awake from staying up so late the night before. As usual, Levi claimed a window seat.

Andi slipped into the wide seat facing Levi and slouched against the window. Mitch tossed their baggage overhead and sat down beside her with a contented sigh. Chad made himself comfortable next to Levi. He stretched out his long legs to fill the foot space between the facing seats. With a yawn he slid his hat down over his face.

The train left the station and picked up speed along the straight valley floor. Andi's eyes immediately closed. Somewhere between waking and sleeping, she heard Mitch talking to Chad.

"She did a good job, Chad. Flint and the *remuda* were not getting along at all. I watched ever since you mentioned it. I didn't want to do it, but when you went down, I had to shift things around. Andi slid into the job as slick as you please. Flint and Levi did fine with the herd too."

Andi opened her eyes a slit.

Chad lifted his hat and peeked at Mitch from under the brim. "Dare we tell Mother? We promised to keep Andi with Cook."

"The bigger question is . . ." Mitch paused. "Dare we tell Andi? If she finds out how well she did wrangling, she'll pester us day and night to go on another cattle drive. We'll have no reason to say no."

A warm glow engulfed Andi. *I did that well? I carried my own weight?* But—she squirmed mentally—did she really want to go on another cattle drive?

Her whole body went limp thinking about it. Working from dawn to dusk, sleeping on the ground, listening to bellowing cows, fighting mosquitoes and mud and dust, nearly drowning, encountering cattle thieves, shootings, more dust, more cattle . . .

No, helping out on another cattle drive did not send prickles of delight racing up and down her arms like it had last month. She popped her eyes full open. "A cattle drive is not as much fun as I thought it would be," she confessed aloud.

Mitch grinned and folded his arms across his chest. "So, you're awake." He winked at Chad.

Chad pushed his hat all the way back and straightened up in his seat. Next to him, Levi cocked an ear to listen. "Gee, little sister, that's too bad," Chad said, scratching at his chin. "Maybe you should come up with another way to celebrate your fifteenth birthday."

A *quinceañera* suddenly sounded like a lot more fun than working herself half to death. But Andi had made her choice. She slumped. "It's too late." A quiet sigh escaped.

"Maybe not." Chad paused. "Suppose Mother granted you an opportunity to choose again. Just what, Miss Carter, would you choose *this* time?"

Andi had no trouble coming up with an answer. She looked at Chad then Mitch. "Would you really talk to Mother?" When they nodded, she said, "I want Melinda to help me pick out the prettiest gown at the dressmaker's. Then I'll invite all my friends to the grandest *fiesta* in the whole valley. *Música! Danza!*" She giggled. "I'll even dance with *you*, big brothers. I want to show everybody—and especially old Sid—that I'm ready to make the transition from little girl to young woman."

Chad and Mitch stared at Andi, speechless. Levi's dark eyes grew round with surprise.

Chad cleared his throat. "Well, that's—"

"Don't get me wrong, Chad," Andi interrupted for the last word. "This doesn't mean I don't want to help around the ranch. But you can tell Justin I've definitely gotten any cattle-drive notions clean out of my head."

Everybody laughed, and Andi laughed the hardest. *A merry heart doeth good like a medicine*, she thought. And it was true. The hardships she'd endured the last three weeks drifted away like the wispy remnants of a bad dream.

Andi wriggled into a comfortable position against Mitch's shoulder, closed her eyes, and went back to sleep with a smile.

Don't Miss the Entire Circle C Milestones Series

Thick as Thieves
Heartbreak Trail
The Last Ride
Courageous Love
Yosemite at Last
Stranger in the Glade